Falling for Jack Frost

MOLLY LIKOVICH

for all the ho ho hoes out there

Winter is coming.

— GAME OF THRONES

Playlist

Winter Moon by Eurotan
Inkpot Gods by The Amazing Devil
Giving In To The Love by AURORA
Conqueror by AURORA
Quietly Yours by Birdy
Tír na nÓg by Celtic Woman (feat Oonagh)
The Whole of the Moon by Celtic Woman
Newgrange by Celtic Woman
The Dawning of The Day by Celtic Woman
As The World Falls Down by David Bowie
Yearning by Elizabeth Teeter
Mary on a Cross by Ghost
Swan Upon Leda by Hozier
Foreigner's God by Hozier
In the Woods Somewhere by Hozier
Walking in the Air by Karliene
Running up That Hill (A Deal With God) by Kate Bush
Love and Anger by Kate Bush
Taxman by Kiki Rockwell
Mine Forever by Lord Huron

Frozen Pines by Lord Huron
Winter Winds by Mumford & Sons
You Missed My Heart by Phoebe Bridgers
Snow & Ice by Sophia Anne Caruso
willow by Taylor Swift
ivy by Taylor Swift
hoax by Taylor Swift

Glossary

- *Kalevala* - epic Finnish poem, similar in style to The Odyssey
- *Haltija* - elf
- *Keiju* - fairy
- *Menninkänen* - goblin
- *Tapio & Mielikki* - God & Goddess of the forest
- *Lemminkäinen* - hero from the Kalevala

Content Warning

This book contains darker topics and explicit sexual content. It is intended for readers 18+ Please visit mollylikovich.com for a full list of content warnings.

CHAPTER 1

Snowfall

There is no use fighting the imminent storm, Mary.

Ghost Girl's words echo throughout the empty museum halls and rattle around in my brain. Back during the early days of my graveyard shifts I would've varied between calling out, "who's there?" like a terrified and idiotic horror movie maiden or mumbling "shut up, bitch," loud enough for her spectral ears to hear.

Now I just don't care. I ran out of coffee two hours ago, I'm running on fumes, and I can just feel a wave of anxiety-induced insomnia coming my way. This always happens around the holidays. I'm so sick of it.

He's here, Mary.

I clench my jaw so hard my teeth hurt as I stave off the overwhelming desire to tell this poltergeist bitch to fuck all the way off. But that's what she wants. The other ghosts that haunt these halls are more chill. They just want to lurk and loom over paintings and tourists for all eternity. Some of them get bored and dissolve; whether they somehow Blue Skadoo into the paintings, or fade into the next life—whatever the hell that may be—I don't know.

But Ghost Girl is relentless. Once she realized I could hear her, she decided to never shut up. I think she was a soothsayer or some shit back when she breathed, but now she's just a pain in my ass whenever the battery life on my airpods runs out and I have to endure her eerie, windchime voice.

I go to the bathroom in the Monet hall and rip off pieces of toilet paper, ball them up, and stuff them into my ears in a feeble attempt at ear plugs. I make my way back to the main security desk to see a shadow banging at the front door. My hand goes to my hip where my regulation taser is holstered— as if that would do any good against an intruder—and go into a fighting stance I learned three years ago at one of those free women's self defense classes. A pretty pathetic combo of protection I must say.

"Mary!" the shadow shouts, banging on the glass some more.

"Fuck," I mumble.

It's Crazy Hettie.

I take my makeshift earplugs out and toss them on the desk before shuffling over to the door.

I don't unlock it.

"We're closed, Hettie."

"He's coming, Mary!"

"Yeah, it's Christmas Eve," I say, not trying to hide my exasperation. "Ho ho ho, Hettie. Go home. I'm working."

I turn to leave but the old woman keeps banging.

"Mary!"

"God, Hettie, what!" I snap. "I don't have time to hear your Old Man Winter tales right now."

"Oh I'm sorry, luv," she says with a snide smirk, "are you very, very busy in there?" She throws her head back and cackles at her weak attempt at a joke. I glare at her. "I'm trying to help you, Mary."

Then she coughs and hacks. I swear this woman was born with a cold.

"Aren't you going to invite a poor, old woman in for a nice cup of hot chocolate?"

"No."

"Come on, Mary. 'Tis the season."

I lay my hand on my taser and raise an eyebrow at her.

"Are you going to quote the Bible next?"

She shakes her head and laughs again. God I hate this woman.

"Did my father send you?" I ask.

She does her best to hide the truth behind her eyes, but she fails. You'd think after all these centuries she's lived she would be better at lying by now.

"Tell my dear old dad that I said he and his prophecy can fuck right off and have a happy new year."

I turn and start walking away. Hettie keeps banging on the door but I ignore her.

"I'm trying to warn you, Mary! He's coming for you! Tonight!"

I stop but I don't turn around. I hate Hettie. I hate my father. I hate that a small part of me believes in all this bullshit. But magic as my father and his followers might be—as Crazy Hettie might be—I will not believe in outright fairytales that I have never seen any evidence of.

She means Jack Frost, Ghost Girl croones across the air.

"I know, bitch! I know!"

I spin back around to face Hettie and scream at her too, I need to let off a little Yuletide rage. But when I look back at the door, Hettie is gone.

"Good riddance," I mutter as I head back to my desk.

When I make it back to my desk further embedded in the lobby of the Boston Museum of Art, I see a book that wasn't there before. I round the corner of my desk and once I am able to make out the title I practically growl in annoyance.

The Kalevala.

Epic Finnish poetry about gods and sprites and other kinds of mythical bullshit my father raised me on. True as some of the creatures in its pages may be (my father and I are living proof) the stories and prophecies it weaves are about as accurate as Grimms' Fairy Tales. I notice there's a bright green sticky note poking out of the pages. I grab the book and flip it open to where the note has marked a passage from Runo 30.

> Frost boy of wicked lineage
> And lad of vicious vapors
> Started out to freeze the ocean
> And to still the heaving billows.
> As he went there on his way,
> As he crossed the countryside
> He bit the leaves off every tree,
> And he stripped the haystalks sheathless.
> When he reached the northern sea,
> Vast and barren stretch of shoreline,
> Right away upon the first night
> Froze the bays and froze the ponds,
> And the shoreline iced up quickly,
> But he did not free the ocean.
> Nor yet still the heaving billows.
> Though the chaffinch or the wagtail
> Is so tiny on the sea,
> Yet its claws remain unfrozen
> And its little heart unfrosted.

Now I *do* audibly growl as I slam the book shut and hurl it across the lobby.

This is all I've been hearing for the past twenty-one years. I was born for this—*bred* for this as my father always liked to say. Fuck that. Fuck him. Fuck *Frost*.

I slump down in my seat, take off my glasses and rest my head on the desk, my blue hair pooling around my head like water. It's Christmas Eve, not exactly a bustling night for art theft so I don't feel even a little bit guilty as my eyes begin to droop. Take that, insomnia.

"Hold down the fort for me, Ghost Girl," I murmur against the fake wood top of the security desk.

You cannot fight the storm, Mary.

"Yeah, yeah, yeah."

Through the blur of my eyelashes I can see snow begin to fall outside.

When I open my eyes again it's well after midnight and the street outside is covered in a thick layer of fresh wintery down. If I wasn't so bitter about this time of year, I would probably be able to appreciate the beauty. I put my glasses back on, lean back in my chair, and sigh. It's close to 1 a.m. Still four hours to go until I can retreat to the comfort of my apartment and deep under the covers in my bed to sleep through the rest of this dreaded holiday.

I decide to go zone out in front of my favorite painting.

Haystacks At Dusk by Monet.

I stand in front of this masterpiece of blur and soft color, swaying back and forth in time with my breathing. When there's only ghosts around, I don't have to worry about masking my stimming. In all the ways this job is a nightmare for my severe ADHD, moments like this are a godsend. The peace paintings bring me is unlike anything else in the world. Give me a Monet, Van Gogh, or Degas over a movie or a good book any day.

I'm so lost in the painting that I don't realize right away that it's snowing again.

Inside.

I snap out of my neurodivergent-daze and look at the ceiling, trying to spot a leak of some kind. But this museum has multiple floors, and the snow isn't coming from just one spot, it's coming down *everywhere.* I look down at my boots to see that it's already sticking to the floor; frosting it like sugar.

"Ghost Girl?" I ask, wondering if she's a freaking elemental now.

For once I want to hear her voice. To confirm that this indoor weather anomaly is her doing and not some weird hallucination I'm having from sleep deprivation. Or maybe I'm still asleep. I pinch myself. Nothing. I spin around, the snowflakes catching on my hair. Flakes start to land on my glasses and I try to use my sleeve to wipe them away, but all I do is add to the collection of preexisting smudges.

Is my dad here maybe? His magic has never manifested into anything this big, but maybe the spirit of Christmas or some shit has gotten ahold of him, ramping his powers up to a ten.

A crackling sound startles me out of my pondering.

Crystal-like ice begins to spread fast across the wall, quickly encrusting the painting frames, and then the floor. It's shooting towards me at a ridiculous speed so I do the only logical thing that one can do in this situation: run.

I only make it a few paces before the speedy ice catches up to me. It slides under my feet, causing me to lose my footing. I make a small sound of fear as I slip and go careening towards the marble floor but a set of hands reach out and catch me at the last minute.

The hands yank me backwards into the firm chest of a stranger. I try to crane my neck to see who it is because something tells me Hettie didn't suddenly grow two feet since we last spoke. Before I can turn my neck enough to get a good look at the figure, they whirl me around to face them.

The sprite-like man towers above me at well over six feet tall. He's thin but not in a gangly way—he's too sleek and composed for such a term. He's wearing long wintery blue pants with a matching tunic. His hair is snow white, his skin so pale it's vampiric, and his eyes glow so fiercely blue it's otherworldly.

Because he *is* otherworldly.

"It's you," I say, trying to maintain my bitchy, bitter cadence from earlier in the night, but the magic death-ice and indoor snowstorm has kind of thrown me for a loop so my voice ends up sounding like a damsel in distress.

He smiles at me, but it's not the kind of warm, jolly smile from cute kids' stories about this Yuletide being. It's more akin to the legends of the viscous Fae. His lips spread across his sharp teeth in a wicked way and his fingers dig in deeper against my arms; his nails pricking at the thin fabric of my uniform.

"You've been expecting me, little will-o-wisp?"

"No."

He smirks again.

"Liar. Come, time to go."

"I'm working," is my incredibly articulate and intimidating response.

He laughs, the sound is far too melodic for comfort. No being should be this ethereal. It's like he's made of light and whimsy and horror all rolled up into one.

"I know you, little will-o-wisp. I know you were not raised in ignorance. It's your twenty-first birthday, your time in this world is up, now you must join me in mine."

I can practically hear my father chanting "I told you so," from his corner of the city.

"I had nothing to do with the bargain," I say, trying and still failing to sound firm.

"I truly do not care," he says, his melodic voice becoming vile. "Your father struck a deal with me a long time ago. I was merciful and generous. I did not need to give you any years here, let alone twenty-one. Now come."

He lets go of my arms but before I can lurch away he snakes one freezing hand up to clamp around the back of my neck. He uses the pressure to push me forward, slipping and shuffling in the most undignified manner across the ice. He looks too lean to be so strong.

He keeps pushing me until we reach the wall where my Monet painting hangs. It's nothing but a sheet of ice now.

"You ruined it," I say softly, sadness creeping into the corners of my voice.

"Do not be so horribly human," he says. "All will be as it was once we're gone."

I guess that can be my silver lining, he didn't ruin a room full of priceless art.

"Why couldn't you just be an art thief?" I mutter.

And then I remember.

My taser.

Before I get a chance to second guess myself on how stupid this is I pull it out of my holster, click the button, and shove it into Jack Frost's side. The vibration of electricity causes his icy skin to crackle and shimmer like fireworks. It doesn't stun him the way it would a human but it does cause him to flinch enough that he loosens his grip on my neck and I use this chance to turn and run.

I only make it a few feet across the room before he tackles me to the floor, my body crashing into the ice. I hiss from the pain as he presses his body against mine, digging his fingers into my hands as he presses them flat against the ice that's now getting painfully cold.

"Stop," I gasp, finding it hard to get a full breath with him crushing my body into the ice.

"Behave," he growls in my ear. "I won't tell you again."

He shifts off of me and I manage to push up onto my knees before I feel his spindly fingers knotted in my hair, and then he tugs. I cry out in shock and pain as he begins to drag me across the floor. My hands go to his wrist that has an iron-clad grip on my hair, the pain stinging and searing through my scalp.

"Stop!" I beg.

He ignores me.

He drags me back to the Haystacks painting and then yanks me right through. In a blur the museum fades away and before I know it, Jack Frost is hauling me across a snowy forest floor.

"Stop it, you fucking bastard! You won! I'm here!"

I hear him chuckle; the sound is sickening.

He finally releases me and my head falls back into the snow. My entire skull feels like bee stings. I reach up to massage my scalp but the frost demon is on me again, strad-dling me and pressing my hands into the ground with his own. He leans over me. His eyes are daggers that pierce my heart over and over. I try to look away but there's something about his gaze that makes it impossible.

"Do you know why you're here, little will-o-wisp?"

"Yes," I say through gritted teeth.

"And do you know who I am?"

"Jack Frost."

He smirks. "Yes, that's your world's cute little name for me."

I glare at him. "Father Winter, The Frost King, Morozko, Pakkanen The Freezer, Father Frost, Raging Asshole—shall I continue?"

His smile widens. He releases one of my hands to grip my chin, making sure I have nowhere to look but his eyes.

"I like you, little will-o-wisp. This will be fun."

I want to curse and scream and kick, but he's not a museum ghost, or a fairytale, he's a walking, talking, *dark* legend that was never supposed to be true. He's just supposed to be another character from my father's bullshit stories and prophecies. My father is only half Haltija. The magic of Finnish elves should've been so diluted by the time it got to me that there was no chance that anything my father predicted for me would ever be remotely accurate.

"I have a name," I say.

"Enlighten me," he replies, my chin still stuck in his icicle grip.

"Mary Ellory Lark."

"Pretty."

"Excuse me?"

He chuckles again. "Did you think I planned to spend all of eternity tormenting you?"

Eternity. That word makes my stomach churn with nausea. It's too heavy. Too untouchable. And I can tell he means it.

"That was the impression I got, yes."

He releases my chin and drags his nails across my jaw and then down the length of my throat. The motion causes me to shiver and I have to fight the urge to gasp from the startling sensation that is, admittedly, not altogether terrible.

"I suppose you'll see it as torment at first. But you will get past that in time. Pain can become pleasure—with practice."

I bite my tongue until it hurts. I want to tell him to fuck off so badly, but my head still hurts from the hair pulling.

He rakes his nails down farther until he reaches the collar of my god-awful long-sleeved uniform polo shirt with the museum logo in the corner.

"Though I *do* enjoy tormenting you already, so hopefully you don't get over it too quickly."

"What?" I ask, my voice coming out far too breathy.

He grins wide this time, flashing me his sharp teeth.

"You heard me, little will-o-wisp."

He leans forward and his mouth crashes against mine. I go still at first and then start to squirm under him, trying to fight the assault but it's no use. He's far more powerful than me, I'm only one-fourth elf and he's a full-blooded deity. He pushes against the seam of my lips with his tongue, trying to invade my mouth but I keep them shut tight, trying to maintain what little fight I can.

"Don't be a spoil sport, Mary Ellory," he says against my mouth.

He moves away from my lips and ducks down to my neck where he drags a slow, icy lick of his tongue from my collarbone up to my ear. Without a thought I arch against his body, gasping in surprise pleasure.

It's just my body reacting. Not my mind. He can't have that. Not ever.

He nips at my ear and I whimper. He laughs, the sound is tinny and awful and wonderful and I fucking hate him.

He shifts over to the other side of my neck and repeats the licking. I can't believe how much my body enjoys this. I use my free hand to try and push him off, but that gets me another growl from his wintery lips. He grabs my wrists in one hand, wrapping his long fingers around them like a cuff. Then he uses his free hand to press against my pussy through the cheap fabric of my uniform slacks.

"Wait!" I gasp.

He laughs directly in my ear as he bites at the skin just behind my earlobe.

"Wait, little will-o-wisp? Not stop? I can move slower."

"That's not what I—"

Before I can finish my sentence he presses two fingers against my mound and drags them up slowly, applying just enough pressure to make me squirm. Even with my pants as a barrier it still feels *too* good.

"No," I moan.

"No, what?" He whispers in my ear before biting me again.

"Too much."

Another laugh. "We've barely begun, Mary Ellory. I have so much more for you, and you will take it all. I know you can."

"I don't want it," I gasp as he continues to drag his fingers up and down the length of my pussy. Even as I say the words my body betrays me; he's barely touching me and I'm already melting under his caresses.

"I can feel how wet you are already, little will-o-wisp. Even with these hideous clothes in the way. Your body wants me."

"You're doing something to me," I whimper, knowing that's not true. He doesn't have that kind of magic. But I *need* it to be true. My body can't be doing this on its own, it has to be influenced because if it isn't...I can't even think about that.

"I control the Winter, Mary Ellory. As much as I would love to control this pretty pussy, those kinds of powers are beyond my reach. However..."

He stops dragging his fingers and instead begins to tap his index finger against my clit with just enough force to feel horribly pleasurable.

"I *can* use my powers on you."

I arch against his hand and cry out as the sudden sensation of ice invades my vagina. It feels as if ice cubes have been shoved up between my folds and deep into my cunt.

"Oh my god," I sob as the cold intensifies.

"Mmm," he murmurs in obvious satisfaction. "Very nice."

He shoots another wave of ice through my pussy and I

gasp louder than before. He uses this opportunity to swoop his mouth back over mine, shoving his tongue into my mouth. I groan as he fucks my mouth with his tongue; his ministrations are rough and freezing and they feel so fucking good.

I hate that I don't hate this.

Without letting up on the icy sensation he's injecting inside me he continues to tap my clit harder and harder. I writhe beneath him wishing he would do more, give me more. I try and fail to remind myself that I shouldn't want this—that I *don't* want this, but his touch is making it a useless endeavor.

As if reading my mind, sensing my doubts, he intensifies the ice inside my pussy and I cry out but he swallows the sound with another violent kiss.

"Please," I say around his mouth on mine; no idea what I'm begging for.

"Want me to make you cum, little will-o-wisp?"

I can't help it, I nod, our lips melding together as I do.

"I think you're still too warm," he says, nipping at my mouth. "Let me help you cool down."

His ice shoots into my breasts, causing my nipples to throb and pucker. I groan and he drinks up the sound, tongue-fucking my mouth once more. The ice continues to pulse in my nipples and pussy until I'm a whimpering, quivering mess. I have never felt so ashamed and undignified and so *needy*. I need to cum and I need it now.

"Jack," I pant.

"Yes, little will-o-wisp, I like how my name sounds when you beg."

"Please," I whimper.

He ramps up his power until the invisible ice in my body has me writhing and screaming. He kisses me again and I tilt my hips up as far as they will go, he's still just tapping my clit and nothing else. I need friction, I need force, I need release.

"Please," I sob again.

He laughs once more and then presses his thumb firmly to my clit and begins to circle it rapidly, all the while keeping his ice pumping through my breasts and cunt. I practically scream from the intensity of the dual pleasures and my orgasm claims me with a violent passion. I come undone underneath the frost demon. I am his to command. His property. His for eternity all because my father made a stupid decision twenty-one years ago.

"Yes," he whispers in my ear. "You *will* be fun to torment."

"You're a fucking asshole," I say. I lift my head up, bite his lip, and tug.

He only laughs as his cold, blue blood coats my tongue.

It tastes like sugar.

This fucker even bleeds beautifully.

"You're fun, Mary Ellory."

He stands up, pulling me up with him.

"Can you walk?" He asks.

"Yes," I grumble.

"So angry," he says, like I'm a child he's condescending to.

"Yeah I just got assaulted by the personification of winter, not my favorite way to spend the holidays."

"Oh don't be so dramatic. Come."

He takes my hand in his and starts walking deeper into the forest.

"Where are we going?" I ask as I stumble after him.

"Home."

"*Your* home," I say.

"You might as well think of it as yours," he says, glancing back at me—those dagger-eyes piercing me once more. "Considering you're never going to see your old home again."

I open my mouth to tell him off but he continues without giving me a chance.

"Get it out of your system now, Mary Ellory, because after the wedding don't think I will be so understanding."

"That back there was you being understanding?"

He yanks me forward until I'm tucked against his side and he can sling one long arm across my shoulders.

"Yes," he purrs in my ear before nipping at me again.

I try to lean away but of course he doesn't let me.

"You smudged my glasses," I say, not able to think of anything else.

He reaches over and plucks my glasses off my face.

"Hey! Those are expensive! Give them back!"

I doubt there's a LensCrafters here so I'm going to have to hope my prescription never changes.

He holds the lens between his fingers and rubs them together.

"Jack!"

"Do shut up, my little will-o-wisp."

He puts my glasses back on and they're suddenly the cleanest they've ever been, not a smudge or scratch in sight.

"I'll remember to take them off for you next time," he says, pinching my shoulder lightly as he does.

"There won't be a next time," I lie.

"Liar."

"Do I get a say in the matter?"

"Of course not. Your father gave you to me to wed and to bed and to keep. You're the price he paid for his gift."

"And it doesn't bother you that I didn't agree to this form of human sacrifice as payment?"

"Were you an actress in the mortal realm? Because your dramatics are quite entertaining. You are not a human sacrifice. I'm not going to cut you up and drink your blood."

"You just want to fuck me and keep me trapped here with you forever."

He shrugs, his arm still wrapped tight around me as we trek through the snow.

"It didn't look like you were having too much fun back there just staring at the wall."

"I was looking at a painting, you ass."

He chuckles. "I can get you paintings to stare at, my bride."

"Don't call me that."

His laugh turns cruel and cold.

"It doesn't matter what I call you, little will-o-wisp. You will be my wife soon enough."

I feel a knot of nerves begin to form in my chest and my heart begins to beat faster. I can feel an anxiety attack coming on and I do everything I can to fight it off.

"Stop it," Jack says.

He slides his arm from around me and takes my hand in his again, but this time he laces his fingers through mine.

"Stop what?"

He looks over at me, those eyes piercing me once more.

"Worrying. It will do you no good, you cannot undo what has been done."

"Take back my father's gift."

"No."

"Why? Because it will kill him? I don't care about that."

He smirks. "No, I wouldn't imagine you would. But I'm not going to take back the gift because that means I don't get to keep you."

"You just met me."

"That doesn't matter."

"Yes it does!" I say, hating how hysterical I sound.

"Stop being boring, Mary Ellory, we're here."

I start to argue again but again he cuts me off.

"Welcome home, little will-o-wisp."

We stand before a small, stone cottage with a garden full of snowbells outside and ivy growing across the doorframe.

"You live here?" I ask in disbelief.

"Santa's workshop was taken."

"Are you making jokes right now?" I ask incredulously.

"Did you think mortals held a moratorium on humor?"

"But you're the King of Winter, shouldn't you have a palace?"

"If I build you an ice palace will you stop being so annoying?"

"Absolutely not."

"Then we keep the cottage."

He pulls me towards the door and I try to ignore how it made me feel to hear him use the word *we*.

The cottage interior is sparse but homey. There is a stone fireplace with a hearth decorated in holly and cinnamon sticks. A small kitchen with dishes scattered across the counter holding tea leaves and various herbs, two armchairs, and a large bed draped with various blue quilts. It looks more like the home of a friendly woodland witch and not an evil sprite.

"I'm not evil, little will-o-wisp."

My mouth hangs agape as he walks over to the kitchen and begins to make fresh tea.

"Can you read my mind?"

"Yes," he says as he strides past me to hang the kettle over the fire.

"Since when is that a frost demon power?"

"It isn't. I can only read your mind when you think so loudly."

"Think loudly?"

He collapses into one of the armchairs by the fire and looks up at me; his eyes a mix of amusement and exasperation.

"You seem too smart to act so dumb."

I bawl my hands into fists and he laughs.

"Come here, little will-o-wisp," he says as he pats his lap.

I shake my head.

He groans. "Mary Ellory, you need to understand now that I don't need to ask you. I can make you do whatever I say, but nothing would bore me more, so stop being dull and come over here."

"You can't make me, you said so outside."

"Did you really forget the feeling of me inside you so quickly?"

He smirks and a wave of ice hits me, rushing through my body with such force it knocks me to my knees. Jack looks down at me, his smirk ever present.

"Come here, Mary Ellory."

I grind my teeth together and glare at him. I try to stand but he shoots more ice through me and I gasp as I fall forward onto my hands.

"Crawl," he commands.

"I hate you," I hiss.

"How novel," he says, boredom lurking in his voice. "Now, *crawl.*"

The floor beneath my hands turns to ice so cold it burns. I gasp again and finally relent. I crawl over to him until I'm seated before him like a pet. He smiles down at me. He reaches out one hand and cups my chin, tilting my head back to look at him. His ice is still thrumming through me with a vengeance.

"Are you cold, my will-o-wisp?"

"Yes," I say through my now chattering teeth.

"Want me to help you get warm?"

Oh my god I hate him so much.

I nod.

"Use your words, Mary Ellory."

"Just Mary."

"Hmm?"

"Just call me Mary."

He begins to stroke his thumb back and forth across my jaw and I can't pretend it doesn't feel incredibly soothing.

"Mary Ellory is a beautiful name."

"I never use my middle name."

"There's no harm in letting your husband call you something special."

"You aren't my husband," I say.

He smiles then reaches his hand back to dig roughly into my hair. He pulls my head back to look further up at him and I hiss from the pain on my still tender scalp.

"Not yet. Now, Mary Ellory, do you want me to warm you up?"

"Yes, Jack Frost," I say through gritted teeth.

He smiles then reaches out his other hand and hauls me across his lap, my stomach pressed against his knees. The air gets knocked out of me as my hands shoot forward trying to find a place on the floor, all the while he keeps his hand knotted firmly in my hair.

"This blue is a pretty color," he says, tugging again on the strands.

"Thanks," I mutter.

He unfurls his fist in my hair for a moment to run his fingers through my hair and I shudder a bit from the gentle, yet intoxicating sensation.

"Spread your legs, little will-o-wisp."

I'm so cold and so infuriatingly aroused again that there's no use in fighting him on this. I shift on his lap to move my legs further apart and he wastes no time in dipping his hand between my thighs, pinching and kneading my sensitive skin. Even with my pants working as a barrier between us I can't deny the thrill his touch sends through me.

"Let's remove these," he says as he reaches under my

stomach to unfasten the button on my pants. "Skin on skin is the quickest way to warm you up."

"No," I say as he begins to tug my pants down my legs. "You stopping your icy onslaught is."

He chuckles but doesn't disagree. He tugs off my boots and then my pants. He slowly traces lines up my bare legs and the backs of my thighs until he reaches my panties. Red lace because it was laundry day so my rarely used lingerie was all that was clean. I hear him hum softly in an approving way as he traces his fingers across the waistband.

"We'll remove these soon," he says.

"Fine," I grumble.

He chuckles softly, sounding appreciative of my sarcasm.

"Behave, Mary Ellory. I can make you feel good."

"Prove it," I say before I can give myself a chance to regret my words.

"Gladly, my bride."

He slips his hand back between my thighs and begins to drag his fingers across the outer lips of my pussy like he did back out in the snow.

"Is that the best you've got, Frost?"

He laughs again and I can practically hear him smile.

"Have it your way, my will-o-wisp."

He yanks my panties down and dips his hand between my folds, wetting them with my undeniable arousal. He begins to prod and probe me, inserting his fingers the slightest bit into my pussy, just enough to drive me insane.

"Jack," I moan against his leg. "Stop teasing me."

"No."

He retracts his fingers completely and returns to just slowly dragging them back and forth across my folds.

"I hate you," I whimper.

"You won't soon. At least for a little bit."

"I sincerely doubt it."

"Hmmm, well that's no good is it?"

He moves swiftly and before I have any time to process what's happening he thrusts two fingers deep inside me, crooking his hand forward just right, hitting my G-spot and causing me to writhe against him, moaning louder than before.

"Oh god," I groan.

He continues to stroke his fingers in and out of my pussy in perfect time, keeping up a relentlessly tormenting pace, refusing to let me cum. I try to grind against his hand and grant myself the sweet relief I desperately need but he won't allow me this.

"Mary Ellory," he says, smoothing the hand that was in my hair flat on my back. "You need to understand something before I make you cum."

"What?" I whine, burying my face against his thigh.

He removes his fingers from my pussy and moves them to my clit where he begins to slowly circle it with the lightest touch. I whimper and he laughs.

"I own you now, Mary Ellory. You are to be my wife and my constant companion in this world. I can hurt you just as well as I can pleasure you. But I decide when. I decide when this pretty pussy gets to orgasm. I decide when you need to be punished. I decide when you need my ice."

"And what do I decide?" I gasp.

There is a pause.

"When to take my cock," he says.

"What?"

He begins to apply more pressure to my clit.

"I won't fuck you until you beg for my cock."

"Great," I say, my voice rife with sarcasm. "So you'll just do everything else."

He removes the pressure from my clit and lands a hard

swat across my ass. I arch my back and cry out from the sweet sting of the slap.

"Yes. Now, do you understand?"

"I disobey you and you ice me, yeah I get it."

He laughs but not in a mocking way for once.

"Good girl. Now you may cum."

He thrusts his fingers inside me once more, this time using three while his thumb circles my clit with fervor and I scream in pleasure as he fucks me relentlessly with his hand. I orgasm so hard it shakes my body but he just keeps pumping his digits into me until a second orgasm, even more brutal than the first, washes over me. Even then he continues finger fucking me. My legs are shaking and my pussy is so tender it's throbbing.

"Jack," I pant. "I can't take any more."

"Nonsense, you have at least one orgasm left in you before the wedding."

He picks up the pace of his hand, shoving his fingers into me and curling against the sweet spot inside my cunt that makes me sob with euphoria. I wish so badly I didn't enjoy this torture but this god forsaken frost demon knows what he's doing in this department.

"What do you think, my little will-o-wisp? Can you cum one more time for me?"

He slows his thrusts to a more shallow, steady rhythm, once again denying me the release he promised.

"Yes," I whisper, my entire body shaking.

"Good girl."

He resumes his fervent motions, his hand fucking me to a completion so intense it feels as if my soul leaves my body for a moment. When he finally retracts his fingers from my cunt I go limp against him, my body completely spent.

He pulls my panties back up my legs, sliding them into place, then he hauls me up so that I'm settled across his lap. His icy eyes bore into mine.

"The sun will set soon and we will go to the sacred tree to be wed beneath the stars."

He reaches up and runs his knuckles down the curve of my jaw. The motion is so gentle it's startling coming from him.

"You will like me soon enough, Mary Ellory."

"I highly doubt that, Frost."

He smirks, flashing his sharp teeth.

"We will just have to wait and see."

CHAPTER 2

Shivers

J ack stands up and saunters out of the cottage leaving me alone in my uniform shirt and red lace panties. I stand there completely dazed. His ice is gone from my body but the confusion and heat of his touch is ever present.

Only a few seconds pass before there's a knock at the door. I quickly look all around for my pants but Jack seems to have somehow made them disappear.

"Hello?" A melodic, womanly voice calls out. "May I come in?"

"Um...no?"

Whoever it is laughs and enters anyway.

A small, slender woman with green skin, flowing violet hair, and gossamer wings stands in the doorway.

"I take it you're Mary Ellory? I'm Cilla."

I nod. I give up, guess I'm going to have to hear my middle name for the rest of eternity.

"And you're a keiju. A fairy."

"Yes," she says. "You know your Finnish folklore I see."

"I'm one fourth haltija."

"Yes, Jack mentioned that."

"Did he also mention that I hate him and don't want to be here?"

She laughs again, the sound is much kinder than Jack's.

"Yes, something along those lines."

"I take it you don't care that I didn't choose to be here?"

"Darling, the foolish choices of humans are no concern of mine, I'm just here to help you get dressed for your wedding."

"Fantastic," I mutter.

Cilla walks to the fireplace and removes the kettle from its hook. She heads to the kitchen and quickly fixes some tea. She brings a cup back to me and holds it out. I shake my head.

"I don't like tea."

"You will like this tea."

I sigh and grab the cup, taking a tentative sip. My eyes widen in shock as the taste of freshly baked, warm, and gooey chocolate chip cookies coats my tongue.

"It tastes like—"

"Your favorite food. Yes. Jack had me bring it over this morning."

"Oh. Wow."

The fact that Jack did something kind to prepare for my arrival stirs something inside of me that I do not have the wherewithal to examine right now.

"Let's get you dressed," Cilla says.

Twenty minutes later Cilla is leading me through the snow even deeper into the forest. The stars are out, shining brighter than any I've ever seen, and the ice in the trees looks like crystals as they catch the shimmers of moonlight.

My dress is ridiculous. Long and silver just like the stars, like Jack's hair. An ornate pattern spans across the bodice splaying out into a thin tulle skirt and train that drags behind me through the wintery down on the forest floor. Cilla painted my face with complicated silver swirls and patterns to match the dress and pretty much everything else in this hellish winter wonderland. I'm barefoot but somehow the snow doesn't hurt my feet, it feels as if I'm walking on a plush carpet. Jack must have used his power to make the snow more bearable for me. He also could've just given me shoes, but I guess this nonsense is more up his alley.

A few more steps and we emerge into a clearing drenched in starlight. At the center stands an immense spruce tree with a pair of faces carved into it. I can tell who they are immediately: Tapio and Mielikki. The God and Goddess of the forest. I hate to admit it but my father's insistence on shoving Finnish folklore down my throat my whole life has actually served a purpose.

Jack stands beneath the tree, his blue tunic and pants exchanged for silvery white ones. His face is painted in the same fashion as mine and there are bits of sparkling ice in his hair.

He is so beautiful.

Fucking bastard.

Cilla leads me up to Jack's side and he takes my hands in his. I keep my gaze trained on the ground.

"Little will-o-wisp, look at me."

Reluctantly I bring my head up to meet his gaze. He smiles, and unlike before it's not taunting or viscous; it's eager. He reaches out and takes my glasses off my face and tucks them into his tunic pocket.

"Don't break them."

He smirks. "I won't. Now, repeat after me," he says.

He begins to speak Finnish. Of course he does. My Finnish isn't as polished as I would prefer but I still can understand what he's saying.

I take you as my mate.

"Are you hoping I don't understand what we're about to say?"

He smiles a bit wider. "I would never doubt your intelligence, my bride. Now, *repeat*."

These are just words. I can say them, they don't need to mean anything.

"I take you as my mate," I repeat in Finnish.

He continues in Finnish. "From now until eternity."

I glare at him and repeat his words back.

His smile turns wicked again. He reaches up and grabs the back of my neck as he leans forward and presses his mouth to mine. I feel the roots of the tree pulse beneath our feet as his tongue invades my mouth, his ice spreading through my body in a sickeningly delicious way. Without meaning to, I groan against his lips as his other hand reaches out and wraps around the small of my back, crushing me against him.

This is not the kind of kiss that is suitable for a normal wedding.

A mortal wedding.

But this is a wedding for immortality. I wonder if I, too, will live forever.

"Yes," he whispers against my mouth, reading my thoughts. "You will. Give me your hands, Mary Ellory."

I don't even have a chance to move of my own volition before he snatches my hands up again.

"This will hurt."

"What?" I breathe against his lips.

Then his ice shoots through my hands in the most brutal way. I scream from the agonizing pain as the ice spreads through my skin and into my veins, infecting me, corrupting me.

"Jack," I whimper.

"Almost done, little will-o-wisp."

I shake and feel tears begin to fall. Just when I think I'm going to black out from the pain, the feeling vanishes. I look down at my hands to see the silver patterns Cilla painted on my face are now etched across the skin of my hands and up my wrists. I look into Jack's eyes in fear.

"What did you do to me?"

He releases one of my hands to run his fingers through my hair.

"I gave you my ice. Your body is frozen in time now, you will never age past twenty-one. You will never die as long as you are by my side as my wife."

"And if I leave you? If I run away?"

"You will die."

My mouth falls agape in horror as his words rattle through my mind. I try to pull myself free from his hold on me but he's too strong.

"You knew. You knew I would never be able to leave."

"Of course I knew. And your fool father knew too when he signed away your life to me. I imagine he thought he was doing you a favor, giving you the same gift I gave him."

I look down at my hands again.

My father's hands look nothing like this.

"I put the ice in his heart," Jack says.

"Stop that," I whisper. "Stop reading my mind."

"You do not command me, little will-o-wisp."

"But *you* command me?" I ask, glaring at him once more. "Is that how this will be forever?"

He shakes his head with a laugh.

"You're cute when you throw a tantrum."

"This isn't a tantrum, this is dread."

He begins to trace his fingers along the curve of my ear, toying with the sensitive skin there.

"You will be young and beautiful forever, cumming around my cock, hand, and mouth whenever you please. No need to act like I've sentenced you to death."

I shake my head, fighting the betraying tears in my eyes. I cannot cry in front of this beast.

"My father had so many children. Why me? I wasn't even born when you made the deal with him. His prophecy was supposed to be nonsense."

Jack laughs at that.

"Is that what he told you? It was a prophecy that I would claim you?"

I hate how he's making me feel like a fool for listening to my father even a little bit.

"Oh no, my darling wife, I wanted the daughter he would have that would be born of ice and poison."

"What does that even mean?"

"Did you ever know your mother?"

"No, she was human. Entirely human. Most of my siblings' mothers were." I gesture to my ears, devoid of pointed edges, something that is usually a sure sign of elfish descent. "My father's diluted elf blood and my mother's entirely human blood is why I can so easily pass for a full human."

He chuckles.

"Why is that funny?" I snap.

"Your mother was not human. She was a peikko. You were a product of the forest goblins' mushroom poisonous aphrodisiac coursing through your father's icy veins. My beautiful bride; half goblin, half elf."

"My father was half elf. There's still a part of me that's human. You can't take that."

"Oh, but I can. Your father lied about that too. Your father was full-blooded haltija. Born a bastard in his ancestral court, he went to the mortal realm to make his fortune, gather his foolish followers, and breed his unremarkable offspring. And then he found me and I commanded him to make you. A frozen heart in return for the perfect bride."

Now the tears fall, I cannot stop them. With every word he speaks he tears away at the world I thought I knew. The father I thought I knew. I hated my father but I thought he was crazy, not a blatant liar.

"Why would you want a bride that's half goblin?"

"Because goblin blood is stronger than elves'. I knew you could withstand my ice in your veins. It is a poison that would kill most races of creatures. I only gave your father a bit in his heart. He stopped aging the day he met me but he will die one day like all the rest of mortal creatures. But you and your icy, poison-bred blood will live forever. You will be mine forever."

I shake my head, my tears falling rapidly now.

"Shh, stop this, little will-o-wisp," he says in a comforting voice as he wipes away my tears. "You will want me in time."

"No, I won't. I will hate you forever."

"There is no escaping me, Mary Ellory."

I could escape him in death. If I ran away back to the mortal world.

"If you think I will let you die, then you're as foolish as your father."

"Stop reading my mind!" I scream, yanking myself free of his grasp and stumbling a few steps back in the snow, nearly tripping over my dress' train in the process.

"I can't, little will-o-wisp. You are my mate. My ice is inside you now. Your thoughts are mine, your body is mine, *you* are mine."

"Fuck you, Jack Frost."

"Yes, that's the idea."

He strides over to me and throws me over his shoulder. I cry out in protest but he ignores me and heads back to the cottage. Eventually I go limp in his arms, too stunned and overwhelmed to fight him. It's not like I can win anyway.

We reach the cottage and he walks in, barring the door behind us, though I don't know who would be fool enough to try and break into the home of The Winter King. He sets me down and immediately backs me up against the wall, caging me in with his arms, his groin practically thrust against mine.

"I hate you," I whisper.

"I know."

He leans in and kisses the skin behind my ear and then begins to make his way down my neck, planting open-mouthed kisses and occasionally nipping at me with his sharp teeth.

"I hate you," I whisper again as one of his hands falls to my waist and grips it firmly to keep me in place.

"I know, tell me again."

He drags his teeth to the base of my neck and bites me hard. I groan and instinctively lean against him.

"I can make you feel so good, my beautiful wife. Every day. I can make you come apart at my command. I can fill you up with so much pleasure you won't be able to stand it. Why do you resist me?"

"Because you're a fucking asshole and I hate you."

He laughs against my skin and licks the bite mark.

"I adore you, little will-o-wisp."

He removes his other hand from the wall and cups my breast, dragging his thumb across my nipple through the thin fabric of my wedding dress. I groan and he laughs in amusement as he repeats the motion over and over again until my nipple is hardened and stands erect. Then he switches so that his hand on my hip cups my other breast and begins to tease and pinch my nipple.

"God," I moan, hating how delicious his touch feels.

"Hmm," he murmurs into the crook of my neck. "What shall I do with my other hand?"

I groan as he tugs on my nipple.

"Tell me, darling wife, what shall I do?"

"I hate you," I gasp as he pulls my nipple even harder.

"I suppose I can figure it out myself."

He reaches down and slides his hand between my legs and begins tapping against my clit like he did earlier, the pressure just light enough to be infuriating.

"God, I hate you!" I whine as I thrust my hips towards his hand.

"Want me to make you cum, dear wife?" He asks as he runs his nose up the side of my neck, blowing icy air in my ear. "Want me to fuck this pretty pussy senseless with my fingers like I did earlier? Or do you want something a bit rougher?"

He brings his hand away for a moment and then slaps my cunt hard, causing me to cry out and my legs to shake. He releases my breast to wrap an arm around my waist, keeping me up as he continues to spank my pussy over the barrier of my dress.

"Jack," I moan. "Please."

"I love when you beg," he says against my ear. "You sound so sweet when you say please."

"I hate you," I say for what feels like the millionth time.

"So I've heard."

Suddenly he tears at the fabric of my dress until it falls away from my body, leaving me in nothing but my red lace panties. He immediately drops to his knees before me as I instinctively cover my breasts with my hands. Upon seeing me do so he looks at me with a hungry, angry gaze. He reaches up and pries my hands away from my chest so that I'm on full view for him.

"Never hide yourself from me, Mary Ellory. You are mine."

I open my mouth to argue, to tell him to fuck off, to tell him I hate him, but then he begins slowly sliding his hands up my thighs and the words get lost in my mouth. He hooks his finger in the waistband of my panties and pulls them down my legs. I step out of them, fighting not to lose my balance. He tosses them aside, likely to never be seen again.

He drags his gaze up my body at an excruciatingly slow pace, drinking in the sight of me, and I have never felt so exposed—so vulnerable.

"You are absolutely stunning."

"Yeah well," I let my head fall back against the wall. "You look fine, I guess."

He chuckles and then grips his hands behind my thighs and moves forward to plant his mouth on my pussy. I cry out as he begins to drag his tongue through my folds, licking me like it's what he was born to do. He digs his fingers into the soft skin of my thighs so hard I'm sure there's going to be bruises there tomorrow. He shifts up so his tongue reaches my clit and he begins to circle it. I moan and jut my hips out against his mouth. He smiles against my pussy and then starts to fuck me roughly with his ice-cold tongue, sending chills throughout my entire body.

"Jack, you fucking bastard."

I whimper as he releases one of my thighs to shove two fingers into my cunt and starts flicking my clit with his tongue once more. His movements are violent and wonderful and my hatred for him battles the passion and heat growing in my chest. He presses his tongue to my clit as hard as he can and begins to circle it, all the while pumping his fingers in and out of my pussy with masterful precision. He curls his fingers forward, hitting my G-spot at the same time he swipes his deft tongue against my clit again and my legs shake as I cry out.

"Do you want to cum for me, dear wife?"

"Yes!" I sob.

To my horror he leans back, removing his tongue and fingers from my cunt and gazes up at me with that wicked look on his face.

"What?" I gasp, trying to get my bearings.

He leans forward on his knees and circles my waist with his long fingers.

"If you want to cum, my darling wife, it must be around my cock. I will gladly torment this pussy all night long with my fingers and tongue, but I will not grant you release."

"You said," I take a big gulp of air, "—that I got to choose."

"And you do," he says with an infuriating smirk. "Either I tease this lovely little cunt all night until you're sobbing and begging me to allow you to finish or you let me take you to the bed and fuck you like a husband should fuck his wife. After that I will happily make you cum over and over again with my mouth and hands. But your first orgasm as my wife—" he moves one of his hands to pinch my clit between his thumb and forefinger and I cry out yet again. "—will be around my cock."

"What if I never let that happen?"

"Then I will never let you cum. And don't think you will be able to finish yourself when I'm not around. I own this pussy as much as I own your mind. You only get to orgasm when I say so."

"I fucking hate you," I whine, letting my head fall back against the wall once more.

"Oh come now, little will-o-wisp. I can make you come apart so beautifully. You've already had my tongue and hand, now take my cock like a good little wife, won't you?"

I groan in frustration and he laughs, because of course he does. I don't want to give in to another one of his commands, but I cannot endure an eternity of this torment. Let him fuck my mind senseless, my body needs relief.

I look back down at him and he raises a mischievous eyebrow in question.

"Fine," I say. "Fuck your wife."

"Good girl."

He shoots up to stand and scoops me up into his arms in one swift motion. He walks me across the cottage and tosses me on the bed. I prop myself up on my elbows and watch as he carefully takes my glasses out of his tunic pocket and sets them on the bedside table. Then he begins to strip away his clothes until he's completely naked.

I can't help but gawk at the sight of his cock.

It is nothing like a mortal man's.

For one, it looks like an icicle, and second, it is *big*. It's long and easily as thick as my forearm. A surge of panic rises in me wondering how it will ever fit without tearing me apart.

"Do not worry, dear wife," he says as he climbs on top of me. "I will make sure you're ready for me."

He reaches down and runs his fingers through the lips of my pussy which are now soaked with arousal for this wintery dickhead.

"Mmm," he groans as he brings his fingers to his mouth and sucks my juices off his skin. "You taste delicious, my little will-o-wisp. I think you're almost ready for me. But let me help you along just a bit more."

And then he smacks my pussy again. I arch my back up towards him and scream from the sudden, sharp sensation.

"Yes," he whispers. "You like it rough don't you, my beautiful bride? Look how wet you get from my palm on your pussy." He spanks me again between my legs. "Your cunt is getting so red. A beautiful rose between your thighs—just for me." He runs his fingers through the tuft of hair over my mound and tugs gently, drawing another whimper from my mouth. "My lovely little wife. Oh the things I have planned for you. We've only just begun." He releases my hair and spanks me several more times in rapid succession.

"Jack, please!" I scream.

He leans down and kisses me. It's as violent as all the rest, his tongue probing my mouth, pulling the groans of desire from me with ease.

"Beg some more, little will-o-wisp. Beg for my cock. You won't get it unless you do."

"I hate you."

He pinches my clit again. I cry out again.

"I thought you wanted to cum, darling wife?"

"I do," I sob.

"Then beg me."

"God, fine!" I open my eyes and look up into Jack's fierce blue ones. "Please fuck me, Jack Frost. Oh darling husband, please impale me with your fat cock and make me scream."

He grins, those sharp teeth glinting in the moonlight streaming through the cottage windows.

"Gladly."

He lines his icicle-dick up with my entrance and right when the icy head slicks through my folds I suddenly stiffen.

"Shhh, little will-o-wisp," he says, leaning down to whisper in my ear. "Relax, you can take me."

"You're too big," I whisper back.

"I won't hurt you."

"You already have."

"And you've liked it. But I won't hurt you now."

I put my hand against his shoulder and gently push him back far enough to look into his eyes again.

"You promise?"

He traces his knuckles down my jaw again. The touch is so tender and gentle it's jarring coming from him.

"Yes, my wife. I promise."

"Alright then," I whisper.

He smiles and then he shifts forward, sinking his thick, icy length deeper inside me. I groan and try to focus on taking deep breaths to get my muscles to relax and let him in. He sinks in another inch and my walls stretch to fit him. I groan from the sensation of fullness so intense it's almost too much.

"My good girl," he whispers in my ear, stroking a hand through my hair. "Look how well you take me."

He pushes in further and my legs shake as I spread my thighs wider to try and accommodate the rest of his cock.

"My beautiful wife, just a bit more. You can take it."

Without thinking I nod and I feel his lips spread in a smile against my neck as he plants a gentle, tingling kiss there.

"Almost there, my dear," he whispers, and then with one final thrust he's seated inside me all the way to the hilt.

His icicle shaft is so cold it's unsettling and he's so thick that the feeling is foreign to me.

"How do you feel?" He whispers in my ear.

"Full."

He chuckles but for once it's not taunting or condescending.

"You take my cock so well, little bride. Now have some more."

He pulls back out almost to the tip and then thrusts forward, slamming his cock back into me, the tip of his icy length hitting something sweet deep within my cunt. I lean my head back against the pillow and moan in delicious pleasure.

"Good girl," he says again.

And then Jack Frost is fucking me relentlessly, slamming his member made of ice in and out of me at a viscous speed. It hurts and it stretches and it freezes and it feels so fucking good. I wrap my legs around his waist and my arms around my neck as his thrusts quicken.

"You feel wonderful, little will-o-wisp," he murmurs in my ear.

He moves his mouth down to bite into the opposite spot on my neck as before and I whimper as I feel him draw blood and begin to lick it up.

"You handle me so beautifully. My ice, my cock; you're perfect for me."

He continues to piston his cock deep inside me, slamming against my inner walls as my muscles clench around him. I feel lightheaded from the pleasure, the heat burning in my belly, begging for release.

"Please, husband," I whisper. "Please let me cum."

"Of course, my wife."

He picks up the pace, his hips thrusting against mine with a violent force until I feel myself reaching the peak of bliss. Right before I topple over the edge he reaches down and pinches my clit once more and I scream as I orgasm, the starlight dripping through the walls and covering our icy bodies as I ride wave after wave of passion. I spasm and cum all over his cock just like he said I would.

Just when I think we're finally finished he flips us over so that I'm straddling him and he shoots me another wicked smile.

"Did you think I was done with you, my darling wife?"

I brace my hands against his chest, shaking my head, no words left to say. He's fucked the sentences from my mouth.

"Oh no," he says as he reaches his hands up to pinch my nipples.

He tugs on the sensitive buds and I tilt my head back and groan.

"Too much," I say as I exhale. "It's all too much."

"Nonsense."

He slides his hands down to my hips and begins to move me up and down on his cock, the icy shaft soothing my swollen pussy as it slides in and out of me. He moves one hand to my clit and begins to flick it over and over again.

"I hate you, Jack," I whisper as I let my head fall all the way back and my eyes close.

"No you don't."

I lift my head back up and look into his eyes. He's still using one hand and his hips to keep me riding him with a steady rhythm. A much gentler fucking than before, but my body still feels weak, the inner walls of my cunt struggling to continue to take him.

"You said you wouldn't hurt me."

He sits up and wraps his cold arms around me, the motion causing his member to press even deeper into me. I groan and bury my face in his neck.

"Too much," I say again.

"Are you hurt?" He asks, softly as he reaches up to stroke my hair.

I shake my head against his neck. He's still moving his hips against mine, his length still penetrating deep.

"Then what's wrong, little will-o-wisp?"

"I told you, it's too much."

"Too much what? Pleasure?"

Instead of admitting to the truth in his words, I bite his neck.

A laugh rumbles through his throat and he tightens his hold on me.

"Oh, my darling wife, how wonderful you are. Hold on to me."

And then he's slamming into me as hard as before. I scream into his neck, biting down on his cold skin again as yet another orgasm claims me. My body shakes against him as I ride out the aftershocks. After a few moments he goes still beneath me and then slowly guides us both to lay flat on the bed with me sprawled across his chest.

"Did you even finish?" I ask.

He begins to gently run his nails up and down my back.

"Of course I did, dear wife. I am no mortal man, I came many times inside the tight walls of your delectable cunt."

"Oh," I murmur against his chest. "It didn't feel like it."

Instead of responding, he slides a hand down between us to stroke my folds again.

"Jack," I groan, burying my face in his chest. He chuckles but doesn't stop. "Give me a moment of reprieve," I say hopelessly.

"Dear wife, earlier you were begging to cum. Are you now begging for me to stop?"

"Is this what you meant by tormenting me?" I ask, turning my head so that my cheek presses flat against his cool skin.

He begins to move his fingers through my folds as if he's strumming a tune on a guitar. This all new sensation sends shivers through my body, causing me to twitch with arousal on top of him. I groan and dig my nails into his shoulders.

"Yes, Mary Ellory. I can't stop now, you make it too fun."

"I hate you."

"No," he whispers. "I don't think so."

He continues his strumming motion between the outer lips of my pussy for so long I lose track of time. The feathering sensation is driving me insane but I don't think I can take his cock again so soon and I doubt he would give it so easily when he's made it clear how much orgasm denial pleases him; so I resign myself to this fate.

Well over ten minutes must pass with his fingers strumming through my folds before he finally inserts two inside me. I groan and twitch again as he does so, but do my best to remain as still as possible.

"I won't beg you to fuck me again," I say softly. "I'm more stubborn than you think. I can take it."

"Mmm," he says, pressing a kiss to the top of my head. "I'm sure you can. Don't worry, I liked fucking you far too much to deprive myself of it anytime soon. But you're so lovely to look at when you squirm."

"You're a real ass, you know that?"

He laughs and kisses my head again, beginning to push his digits deeper inside me.

"Alright, my wife, I'll pull one more orgasm from this

pretty pussy of yours and then we will rest. Tomorrow the torment can begin anew."

I hate the fact that more of this doesn't sound terrible to me.

"But tell me," he says, retracting his fingers and returning to the infuriating feathery strumming motion, "who does this pussy belong to?"

"You're a dick."

"We're not going to bed until you say it."

"You, Jack. It belongs to you."

He inserts one finger into me and I try to swallow a moan, not wanting to give this smug bastard of a husband anymore satisfaction.

"And who owns your mind?"

Another finger.

"You," I breathe as he begins to move his fingers faster and faster.

"And who owns *you*, Mary Ellory?"

"You, husband."

He shoves two more fingers into me and I whimper in shock as he nearly fists me to completion. I cum violently, my body spasming as I orgasm yet again—so many times this night that I've lost count.

"Come, wife," he says, hopping out of bed and holding his hand out to me.

I turn my head to the side and look at his upturned palm —still sticky with my arousal—and back into his eyes.

"Haven't you fucked me thoroughly enough to last three wedding nights?"

He chuckles. "That I most certainly have, which is why it's time for a bath before bed."

"I am not a child."

"No, little will-o-wisp, but you are mine and I take care of what's mine. Now, up."

I know by now I can't win against him so I sigh and take his hand. He leads me through a small back door of the cottage outside to where a small hot spring is nestled in a grove of trees, untouched by the snow.

"Come," he says.

I slowly lower myself into the hot water, doing my best not to hiss with pleasure as my body sinks deeper. Jack gets in behind me and already has a soft cloth lathered with a sweet, berry-scented soap in his hand.

"Mary," he says, gesturing for me to offer myself to him yet again, just for something less sexual this time.

I want to insist that I can bathe myself, but when he calls me 'Mary,' something inside me stirs that I can't ignore and it becomes even harder to obey him than usual.

I shift nearer to him in the water and tentatively hold out my arms for him to wash. It's the first time I get a good look at the new intricate swirls of ice that travel through my veins and up my arms—tattooing me permanently as his.

Jack notices my enraptured gaze and gently rubs his thumb across the inside of my wrist as the other hand continues to gently rub the cloth up and down my arm.

"You will get used to them."

I look up at him. "Have you had other brides?"

"I told you, full-blooded elves and humans couldn't withstand my ice. I needed your goblin blood."

"And how do you know that?"

He holds my stare but says nothing.

"You've killed brides before, haven't you?"

"You don't need to say it like I did it on purpose."

He releases my arm and moves to the other to repeat the washing process.

"What if I died from the ice?"

"That would have been unfortunate."

His voice is cold and unfeeling—almost sarcastic. Of

course. I need to keep my wits about me and remember that he is the equivalent of a God and if my father successfully taught me anything about folklore of any kind it is that Gods do not care for the whims and emotions of mortals.

He wanted a woman he could trap and fuck for eternity. That is all.

And now his ice in my veins ties me to him.

If I leave him I will die.

Or so he says. But he's a trickster and a liar—at least that's what the legends say—so maybe that's a lie too; a fear mongering tactic. Maybe I can escape and get back to my life in Boston. Back to the paintings and the comfortingly eerie museum ghosts. Back to running water and electricity. Back to a real life.

"Did you forget so soon, dear wife, that I can read your thoughts?"

"How?" I snap as he begins to wash down my chest and stomach. "How are you able to do that? I've read all about you and mindreading is not a talent you're meant to possess."

He smirks and motions for me to turn around so he can wash my back. I reluctantly comply.

"You were promised to me in every way. Mind and body."

"And were you not promised to me in return? Why can't I read your thoughts?"

"You can if you try."

I spin around the water and look back up into his taunting eyes.

"Go on, my little will-o-wisp. Try."

I take a slow breath and try to focus. I close my eyes, searching through the energy in the air for something akin to his voice. It happens quicker than I thought it would, amidst the sound of the snow softly falling around us I hear clear as a bell: *I want to bury my cock deep into your tight ass.* My eyes shoot open and with both hands I shove him. He chuckles in amusement, his arms reaching out and pulling me to him.

"Now we are truly entwined, little will-o-wisp."

I shove against him again but it's no use.

"I want you out of my head," I say.

"I don't care."

"Why are you so cruel to me?"

He snakes a hand up my spine to cup the back of my neck, forcing my gaze to remain steady with his.

"I am not."

I scoff. "So this is what kindness looks like on you?"

"Yes. Do not expect me to act like a human man."

"And what of elves and goblins? Are they all as wicked as you?"

"The ones in these realms perhaps. You know only of your father's bastardized world in the human realm. But this is where you belong. Your blood is purely magic, and it is rare magic at that. What good was it to keep it all hidden beneath ugly clothes in an empty museum?"

"I liked the museum," I mutter.

He begins to lightly trace patterns across my back.

"What was the painting you were staring at?"

I don't want to tell him things about me. I don't want us to be close in any way outside of this stupid bargain I had no say in. But after only one night, I can see how adamant my new husband is in his desires. There is no chance he will let anything go once he's decided he wants it.

"Haystacks by Monet. It's my favorite painting."

"Do you paint?"

"No. I just like to look at them. It helps."

He adds more berry-soap to his hands and reaches up to wash my hair.

"Helps with what?"

"The boredom."

"Of your job?"

"Of everything. But not just the boredom, the chaos, the lack of focus, the need to latch on. If I stare at a painting—especially one as wonderfully messy as Monet's—then it's easier to ground myself; to not let my racing thoughts get the best of me."

His fingers feel good in my hair as he gently massages the soap into my roots. I do my best not to arch against him in pleasure.

"Do you feel this way often?"

"Yes. I have ADHD."

"Is that a human ailment?"

I huff in annoyance. "No, it's just an issue anyone with a brain can get. It's a learning disability. And I didn't want to tell you about it so don't be a dick now that you know."

He finishes scrubbing and dips his hands down to cup water to rinse out my hair.

"Why didn't you wish to tell me?"

I shift against him as he wrings out the remaining water from my now damp hair.

"Because you're a jerk and now you're going to make fun of me."

"For having a chaotic mind?"

"Yes."

He leans forward and presses a gentle kiss to my shoulder.

"There is nothing wrong with a little chaos. Come, let's go to bed. You need rest."

CHAPTER 3

Dewdrops

I wake sometime later, naked and smelling like berries, next to my husband. Jack Fucking Frost. I was just a bit hopeful that it was all a dream. But the universe isn't that kind. After twenty-one years as my father's daughter, this much I know for certain.

I look at Jack's undeniably handsome face and let my gaze wander down his defined, lithe chest and torso, and then my eyes stop their exploration at the sight of his morning wood. Or morning ice, rather. It's so big and thick and I just can't believe that it fit inside me only a few hours ago. Will I be able to take him again? He's surely going to expect me to but I still feel a bit sore from last night's chaotic coupling and seeing his erection before my eyes with nothing but the sheet hiding it from my view, it's hard to imagine enduring that again. No matter how good it felt.

I need to get another look at it, maybe last night's frenzy had me misjudge the size and girth. He's still asleep, he will never notice. I reach out slowly to pull back the sheet when one of his hands shoots out and latches onto my wrist.

"Careful," he says, still laying down, eyes still closed. "Don't start something you can't finish."

I flex my wrist in his grip but he doesn't relent.

"The only thing that keeps me from finishing is you."

He laughs, the sound like windchimes, and sits up to capture my mouth in one of his possessive kisses. His free hand knots in my hair at the nape of my neck, holding me firmly pressed up against him, his icy body colliding with mine.

I half expect Jack to shove me down and take me right away but he breaks the kiss and slides out of bed.

"I have work to attend to, darling wife. I will return in a few hours."

"What?" I ask, confused.

What the hell does his work even entail? Creating snow storms? Making roads icy? Casting magic spells to bring snowmen to life?

He slips on some (tight) black pants, a loose white shirt, and a royal blue cloak. He looks like he stepped out of a vintage romance novel.

"I am not going to bring any snowmen to life while I'm away. I promise you this."

He winks and then saunters out the door, leaving me alone.

I sit still and listen until the sound of his boots crunching through the snow is distant and then get out of bed and begin looking for clothes I can wear. This may be my only chance to escape.

I've barely made it across the floor when the door begins to open. Thinking it's Jack I don't bother to cover myself but to my surprise it's Cilla who walks through. I quickly dart back to the bed and wrap myself in the sheet. Cilla just laughs at my modesty.

"I brought you some clothes," she says as she deposits a

large, wooden box on the armchair that just last night sat Jack as he took me across his lap to torture me. I feel a warmth in the pit of my belly at the memory.

God damn it.

"Do you need help dressing?" She asks.

"Tell me about my husband."

She smirks at my bluntness. "Of course, Mary Ellory. What do you wish to know?"

"Is all the folklore about Jack Frost true?"

She shrugs. "A great deal of it."

I sigh in frustration, the fairy smirks.

"So he was summoned by a farmer to freeze Lemminkänen's ship and crewmen but Lemminkänen stopped him by holding him in a fire and threatening to send him to the House of Summer?"

Cilla raises a playful eyebrow. "He was summoned to freeze the ship."

"But Lemminkänen didn't stop him, did he?"

"Do you think a silly hero could defeat your husband? Have you not yet felt his ice?"

I dig my hands into the sheet as I try to keep my face blank. "Yes, I have."

"That was just him playing. He could've killed you in an instant if he wanted to. He kills all the time. Winter kills. How many deaths happen in your realm in the cold months from cars sliding on black ice or careless children falling through ice on a lake to drown a frosty death."

"Shit," I whisper.

"It's not all taunting and games with him. He is the King of Winter. He is Pakko the Freezer. He makes sure winter arrives and wreaks its havoc and if he is summoned by a mortal being foolish enough to bargain with him, well—" she nods at me, "—you see how that turns out."

"I was right," I say. "He is a fucking bastard."

At that Cilla laughs. "Indeed. What is it that silly Finnish poem says about him?"

"The Kalevala?"

"Yes."

I shrug, trying to act like I haven't read the damn thing over a dozen times.

"I don't remember exactly. Something along the lines of he was nursed as a baby with venom instead of milk and rocked to sleep at night by the harsh winds instead of by a mother."

"Yes, that sounds about right."

"So what? He's an asshole with mommy issues?"

Cilla just laughs at me again then turns and leaves without saying another word.

I am alone in my husband's house.

I open the box Cilla brought and inside I find several dresses that look like something fit for a Renaissance Faire. It will be hard to run away in stays and a long skirt but Jack's pants are too long for my short frame and Jack has done away with my museum uniform so I sigh and don my damsel in distress attire. I find a cloak on the back of the door that matches his in its royal blue shade. I fasten it around my throat, retrieve my glasses from the bedside table, and tug on some boots I find beneath the dresses.

I make my way back through the forest to the clearing he brought me through last night. I try to find the portal back to the human realm. Surely one must exist. I highly doubt Jack Frost can create interdimensional travel at the tip of his finger. Even if the painting is gone, the portal must still be there. It has to be.

I reach the clearing and to my immense relief I can see a slight shimmer in the air where the portal is. I bunch my dress in my hands and start walking towards it.

Going somewhere, dear wife?

Before I can even spin around to see him, Jack clamps a hand down over my mouth and drags me back, slamming me up against his body.

"You just can't behave, can you?" He murmurs in my ear.

I mumble against his hand and he chuckles. I resort to biting him and he finally removes his hand so I can speak.

"You didn't say I couldn't go for a walk."

He laughs into my hair then spins around and presses me up against a nearby spruce, taking my wrists in one of his hands and pinning them above my head as his other hand wraps around my throat and squeezes lightly.

"Why are you such a brat, Mary Ellory?"

"I'm not."

"I told you that you would die if you left this realm without me. Do you find me so repulsive that you would rather die than stay here?"

I can't answer that. If I say "yes," then I know I'm lying but how am I supposed to admit that I would choose eternity as his over a peaceful death?

"I was just going for a walk," I insist.

I try to move but he keeps his hold on me firm, squeezing my throat a bit tighter.

"I can hear your thoughts, my little lying will-o-wisp." He thrusts forward, rolling his hips against mine. "Maybe I need to fuck some more obedience into you."

"Maybe you need to fuck off," I say, trying to put as much venom into my words as I can muster with his hand clasped around my throat.

His lips curve into a wicked smile.

"Want to play a game, Mary Ellory?"

"Excuse me?"

"Pick a word," he says, ignoring my question. "A word you like. Any word."

"What are you talking about?"

He leans in and nips at my ear, causing me to gasp in surprise.

"I said," he hisses in my ear, "pick a word."

"Monet," I say without thinking.

He laughs softly and presses a gentle kiss to my throat before standing up straight.

"Monet," he repeats, "means *no.* Do you understand?"

I look into his blue eyes—eyes that burn with every glance. I hate how easily his icy fire is already consuming me after only a day.

"Monet means no," I say.

"Good girl."

He releases me and steps back.

"I will give you to the count of ten."

"What?"

"*Run.*"

"Jack—"

"One."

I take off running through the snowy woods as his melodic voice chants out his counting behind me. If I were smarter I would stop and scream "Monet" at the top of my lungs without letting this continue, but I must admit that a small part of me wants to be dominated and punished. I want to fight back without fear of death or torture or hatred, but no matter what I do to Jack it ends in him laughing and smiling. If I can unleash my rage and my fight and the only conse-quence is an icy cock, well then...

"Ten!" He calls out.

I am not nearly far enough away, my stupid old-timey getup making me jog at a ridiculously slow pace.

I hear Jack's heavy footfalls as he runs after me and I fight the overwhelming urge to look back over my shoulder at him like a girl on the cover of an old gothic novel. But this is a game, and all games have winners. Winners don't back down.

I keep running until my breath is tight in my chest and my cheeks are red, that's when he tackles me. I scream as we tumble to the ground, our bodies thumping against the snow. Jack immediately reaches around for my glasses. He plucks them off my face and sets them aside in the snow.

I use this opportunity to twist underneath him and kick him in the stomach. He grunts softly and I grin as I try to get back up and crawl away. He doesn't even give me the chance. He grabs my ankles and drags me back in the snow as I continue to yell and kick like a madwoman.

"My beautiful wife," he says, slamming me facedown in the snow again.

He wedges his knees between my thighs to pull them apart, then he reaches one hand around to choke me while the other bunches up my dress.

"You need to learn to behave, dear wife."

"Fuck you."

He laughs as he sticks a finger roughly into my already wet pussy. I groan at the admittedly welcome intrusion and his amused laughter loudens. He adds another finger and begins pumping them in and out of me at a violent pace as I writhe and groan beneath him, and all the while he keeps a firm chokehold on my throat.

"I love this cunt. I intend to invade it every day for the rest of our lives." He leans down and whispers in my ear. "Would you like that?"

Yes!

"No, you fucking bastard!"

More laughter.

"You will learn to love me, my darling wife."

Now I'm the one who laughs. I think my next words at him instead of speaking them.

It's not as though you love me.

I wait for his snarky answer but he doesn't give me one, instead he removes his fingers from my pussy and starts spanking my inner thighs. I scream again, wiggling in the most undignified way beneath him.

"You can stop this any time, my dear," he reminds me in a chiding voice that makes me want to punch him. "Just tell me who your favorite painter is."

"God, fuck you!"

He laughs and makes his spanks harder.

"Jesus Christ, Frost! Just fuck me already!"

He stops his spanking suddenly. He switches his grip to the back of my neck so that he's pressing my face down in the snow. He flips my skirt up all the way and I soon feel the head of his icy cock begin to press through my folds.

"My beautiful wife," he murmurs.

Then he slams his huge member into me with one, awful, wonderful thrust, and I scream louder than I ever have before during sex. He groans in pleasure as he begins pumping his cock in and out of me, his grip on the back of my neck so firm that I can barely move. He begins using his free hand to smack my ass as he pounds into me and I soon have no choice but to go limp and give myself over completely to his aggressive passion.

Say Monet, you idiot, I keep telling myself.

I could. I really could.

"Go ahead, dear," he taunts. "Say it."

But I can't. My orgasm is so close and being fucked like this feels so good.

"You will never be able to make me behave," I pant out between his thrusts. "No matter how roughly you fuck me. Or how many times."

His grip on my neck tightens and his thrusts become

somehow even more violent, his hips slapping against mine so hard I can already feel the bruises forming.

"You are mine, Mary Ellory. You admitted so yourself last night. Now beg your husband to make you cum."

All games have winners.

"No."

There is a hesitation in his movements and it fills me with a tiny bit of pride. Let the Frost Demon see that his bride is not so easily brought to heel.

He pulls out of me and flips me over as he cages me in with his arms.

"Do you think you've seen the worst of me yet, little will-o-wisp? I am The Winter King. How many people has history lost to the brutalities of winter? How many storms have ended lives? How many lovers have come together in passion when snowed in, encapsulated by ice? And that's just the humans—the realm of the unknown? Of *our* kind? We are all wicked and I am worse than most. Your father damned you when he sold you to me and I do not care that you had no choice in it. I am giving you a choice now."

I take a shaky breath.

"It's not the one I wanted."

"I don't care about that either. Now, my dear wife, either say your word or beg for my cock."

"Fuck you, Frost."

That horrible smirk tugs at his lips and I don't know if I've made a mistake or a wonderful move in this snowy game of chess.

"Alright, wife."

He gets up, pulling me after him. He plucks my glasses from the snow and slides them back up my nose. Then he wastes no time in throwing me over his shoulder like he did after the wedding. I don't fight him this time, I know there's no point. I could say Monet, but I don't. Because I'm insane now, apparently.

We reach the cottage and he deposits me on my feet once we're inside, barring the door behind us.

"You're the one who left me alone," I say as he turns around. I need to get ahead of this before he starts in on me again. I need to show him that I am not a girl who is easily cowed.

"Yes," he says.

He grabs my shoulders and spins me around. I can't hide the gasp in my throat.

They're all here in the cottage.

Haystacks by Monet. The entire series.

I turn back around to look at Jack, his eyes are completely devoid of any obvious emotions.

"You...why..."

"Well, you didn't tell me which one you liked best and I didn't know the man had painted thirty of the same bloody haystack. So I figured you could pick your favorites and tomorrow I'll return the rest."

I just stare at him, dumbfounded into silence. This is, without a doubt, the best Christmas present anyone has ever given me.

"Jack," I breathe, no idea what to say.

He shrugs like it's no big deal that he just committed massive art theft for me.

"I told you I would bring you paintings."

"I don't know what to say."

He closes out the space between us and wraps his hands around my waist, pulling me in close.

"You say thank you my darling husband and then you shut up while you take your punishment for disobeying me and trying to escape back to your pitiful human realm."

All games have winners and this fucker just beat me. Again.

"Thank you, Jack," I say.

I press my lips together and wait for him to do his worst.

A beat of silence passes between us. He laughs, shakes his head, then hauls me across the cottage and throws me down on the bed. He removes my glasses and sets them aside.

"On your stomach."

For once I do as he says without argument.

He flips up my skirt again so that my bare ass is exposed— old timey outfit did not include panties (figures). I hear him walk away and when he returns he climbs onto the bed and straddles me.

Then I feel his finger tap my asshole.

"Jack," I shift nervously.

He presses a palm to my back and gently presses me back down.

"Relax, dear."

He gently begins to circle the outside of the opening without ever entering it.

"I can't," I whisper, embarrassing fear filling my voice. "I've never—"

"I won't hurt you," he says, the same words he said last night before impaling me on his cock.

"This is a punishment though," I say.

He continues to circle the entrance, applying a bit more pressure with each swirl across my tender skin.

"Surely you can tell by now that all my punishments are fun."

"What if I hate it?"

"Then tell me."

"And you'll stop?"

"I'll stop."

I feel cold lube on my asshole and I gasp from the sensation as Jack uses it to coat my opening before gently pushing a finger inside. I gasp and arch against his hand from the foreign intrusion. I don't hate it, but I have never felt anything like it and I have no idea what to do with this new sensation.

"Good girl," he murmurs in appreciation as he works in another finger, gently stretching my ass to soon accommodate something bigger.

"Now," he says, removing his fingers leaving me feeling suddenly horribly empty, "—this is your punishment."

I feel something else press between my ass cheeks.

"Jack," I say again in fear.

This time he runs a hand gently through my hair to soothe me.

"It's alright, little will-o-wisp."

He squirts more lube onto me and then begins to insert the butt plug.

"Relax, my dear."

I do my best to take deep breaths as he pushes the foreign object deeper and deeper inside me, the fullness almost overwhelming. Once it's fully seated inside my ass he does something that truly shocks me:

He pulls down my skirt and gets out of bed, bringing me up with him.

"What are you—"

"I have work to attend to. Some that involves you." He puts my glasses back on me then takes my hand in his. "Come."

"Jack! The...the—"

"I will remove it tonight and replace it with my cock."

"I can't wear this while we—"

He starts walking, dragging me after him as the butt plug moves with me, the sensation that shoots through me is odd and far too satisfying.

"Jack, I can't."

He stops in the doorway and looks at me, his hand still holding mine.

"Do you have any specific word you want to say to me, wife?"

This fucking bastard.

"No, husband."

He smiles.

"Then you will wear it."

"I hate you," I say, but even I can feel the smile that desperately wants to tug at my lips.

I will not fall for this man. This being. This creature.

He smiles wider and tugs me after him.

We walk deeper into the forest and past the tree where we were married just last night. It already seems like a lifetime ago. His hand is still holding mine, his thumb lightly rubbing across my wrist.

"You know I have to eat, right? Not just magic cookie-tea."

"The tea tasted like cookies to you?"

I groan and he laughs again. He pulls me closer, wrapping his arm around my shoulders just like he did yesterday.

"What kind of cookies?"

I ignore him and look straight ahead but he just squeezes me closer, playfully. I hate it. I love it. I hate that I love it.

"Little will-o-wisp, what kind of cookies?"

"Chocolate chip, okay? Congratulations, you know something else about me."

"Yes, how horrid for a woman's husband to know what she enjoys."

"So you know I like cookies and paintings, big deal."

"True," he says as he begins to rub his thumb back and forth across my shoulder. "I also know you like to be spanked, and pretend that I'm forcing you, and you love my big, thick cock deep in your tight cunt."

"God, you are so vulgar."

He leans down and nuzzles my neck, his breath cool against my skin.

"What is a bit of vulgarity between a husband and wife? Besides, am I wrong?"

"No, you fucking asshole, you're not wrong."

He bites my earlobe and laughs in amusement at my soft mewl in response.

"I still need to eat real food," I insist as he straightens back up. "Using your ice to make me immortal doesn't erase the fact that I was still born mortal. I'm not some magical, endless being that can sustain itself on snow."

"You may not be endless but you are magical. And yes I know you have to eat. There will be food where we're headed and there will be more food at the cottage when we return. I had the kitchen stocked before you arrived."

"Then why didn't you feed me last night?"

"We were a bit preoccupied."

He pinches my shoulder and I do my best to ignore him.

"I thought there would be punishment when we returned?"

He reaches his arm down and lightly spanks me right over the end of the plug. I yelp softly and grab onto him. He drags his hand back up to wrap around my shoulders again.

"This is the punishment, little will-o-wisp. When we get home we play. But first we have to work."

"Are there snowmen in need of coming to life? Did you run out of top hats?"

He laughs again. I shouldn't like that I can make him laugh. But I do. Fuck I do. I grew up surrounded by my father's followers who saw me as nothing—less than nothing. Even my brothers felt the same. My father made it clear from as early as I can remember that I was bred to be sold so that he could be powerful in a realm that wasn't his. Getting out and into my mundane, little life was the only reprieve from his bullshit and abuse there had been. And even though I didn't really believe in Jack Frost, I was still always hesitant to jump into a relationship of any kind with any gender because what if it was all true and the fairy tale swooped in to steal me away? Then I would be heartbroken and enraged.

Now I'm just enraged.

Except I'm not even that.

I feel pathetic that after less than twenty-four hours I already feel more at ease with this insane man. I shouldn't. I'm his toy. That's all.

"You are not just my toy."

Fucking mind reading.

He smirks. "Yes, fucking mind reading."

We walk a bit further and I can see other Fae Folk up ahead in a bigger clearing than the one we were married in. Before we cross through the threshold to see whoever these people are, Jack leans down and speaks directly in my ear.

"Be good, little will-o-wisp." He straightens up, takes my hand, and marches us forward. "Evening all," he calls out coolly as he strides into the clearing.

The other Folk part like the sea for him. He is no God, but this is his domain. Surely he must hold some command over them. He is The Winter King after all. I don't know where I fit into all of this so I remain standing at the outskirts. He waltzes all the way to the spruce that stands at the far end of the clearing. A crown hangs off a branch and he plucks it and drapes it across his head as if it were just a hat and not a vital marker of his station.

"Is it true, Frost?" A shorter Fae (perhaps a keiju?) snaps from the front of the pack. "Did you finally marry the mortal?"

"I did!"

Jack sounds genuinely proud of this declaration—a talented actor.

"But she is mortal no longer. Mary Ellory Lark!"

My head snaps up at my name. He cannot be doing this.

"Come here, my love."

I try to not show any outward reaction to his words. I am not his "love." This is just a show.

It's not just a show, he whispers in my mind and I have to fight even harder to keep myself from giving anything away.

"Come, darling wife, and show the people of my forest what I've done to you."

Walk forward, little will-o-wisp.

I clench my jaw, trying to keep my head high but I don't move a step.

You know I can't.

You walked all the way here.

It was just us, I hiss back in my mind.

Everyone is staring at me.

It will be just us again soon, now come.

He puts more emphasis on the last word and I hate the way it starts a fire in my belly. I hate that I like being bossed around by this endless creature.

I exhale softly and shuffle my way down the aisle of Fae, doing my best not to meet anyone's eye or walk too much like a duck, but the plug in my ass shifts and presses with every step. It's almost unbearable and all I can think about is Frost fucking me senseless again and again like he did last night.

Oh don't worry, my dear wife, I will.

Get out of my head.

Never.

He smiles at me on the last word. Another thing I shouldn't like—that we now have a secret communication only we know about.

I reach his side—finally—and he takes my hands in his. He gently brushes aside my cloak and then pushes up the sleeves of my dress, showing my ice-stained arms for his people to see.

"Behold!" Jack shouts. "The new Winter Queen!"

"What?" I ask in surprise.

He looks at me, grins, and winks, then looks back at his subjects. There is a moment's silence and then they're all cheering.

Long live the Winter Queen! They chant over and over.

"Seppa!" Jack calls out.

I look behind me to see who he's addressing and a gorgeous Elvish person comes into view. They wear similar garb as everyone else seems to in this world; all shades of white, blue, purple, and the occasional dark green—winter colors for a winter people. Their hair is a shade of seafoam green, and their eyes glitter gold. They smile at me as they hold out something before them.

A pillow with an item placed on top of it.

A crown.

"My Queen," they say as they bow their head before me.

I look down at the crown, aghast. It looks like something from a fantasy novel. It's silver and sparkling, and intricate as hell. Endless weaving patterns of icicles and snowflakes. It looks too fragile to even touch. I look at Jack, he's still holding my arms. He smiles and it's genuine, his normal playfulness is gone and in its place there appears to be pure, unadulterated joy.

Jack releases my arms and steps closer to the Elf called Seppa. Seppa holds the pillow before their king. Jack grins and nods his head to them as he takes the crown. He turns to face me again.

Bow just a bit, my dear.

I do as he says inside my mind. As I do I can feel him place the crown on my head.

Stand, my beautiful wife.

Again I obey.

He's smiling at me, I can't fight it. I smile back. The other

Folk are still cheering for us. They keep cheering as Jack cups my face in his and pulls me close to place a passionate kiss against my lips. I gasp softly as he plunders my mouth with his icy tongue and the Folk keep hooping and hollering. When Jack pulls away from me he still keeps one hand pressed gently to my face.

"Food and drink!" He says. "Tonight we celebrate my new bride and your new queen!"

The Folk cheer again and then the festivities begin. Within seconds tables and chairs and instruments and *food,* glorious food has appeared. I don't stop to think about the crown on my head or the plug in my ass as I make my way to the table lined with desserts and delights.

Jack follows me, sliding his hand down from my face to take hold of my hand again. He comes up beside me and takes the gold plate from my hand and begins to fill it for me. He adds a cup of wine and guides me over to a chair in the corner. I'm about to get pissed at him since he knows I can't sit, but instead he sits down and reaches out for me, positioning me on his lap in a way that isn't completely maddening. But I still groan softly from the pressure and fullness. He chuckles in my ear as he nips at my neck.

"I want the punishment to be over now, husband."

"But it's so fun, wife. What will we do when it's done?"

Fuck me.

He bites on my neck a bit harder and I practically choke on my wine as he does.

"I will. Many times."

"Is this food like in the stories? Faerie fruit and all that Goblin Market stuff?"

"No, little bookworm, we aren't in Faerie, we're in the Winter Forest. This is my domain, I would not allow anything here that could hurt you."

"You're here," I taunt, leaning back against him.

He grips my thigh roughly.

"I only hurt you the way you like."

I can't help it, I grind against him, but then Seppa is suddenly standing before us. My eyes go wide but Jack just grins and laughs as usual.

"I wanted to formally introduce myself," they say. "My name is Seppa. I am your husband's Hand."

"It's nice to meet you," I say. "Do you help with all the magic snowmen?"

Jack pinches my thigh playfully and Seppa smiles.

"Yes, something like that. I wanted to tell you, my Queen, that if there is ever anything you need that your husband cannot provide—*anything*—feel free to come to me."

Seppa's gold eyes glow passionately as they bow to me and turn to walk off.

"What the hell was that?" I ask Jack.

"I think Seppa wants to fuck you."

I almost choke on my wine. "And you're not...mad about that?"

With how insane and possessive he is I had just assumed he was the whole "touch her and you die" type.

"I am," Jack says, reading my mind yet again. "If you don't like the idea of Seppa touching you or even how they spoke to you, I will go over there and freeze off one or two of their fingers."

"Jack!" I slap his leg and he grins. "The only person I can ever even consider approving of you doing that to is my father."

Jack's expression is suddenly serious.

"I would gladly kill your father for you, little will-o-wisp."

"I was kidding."

"No, you weren't."

No I wasn't.

Jack slides his hand across my thigh, getting way too close to my pussy for how public the setting is.

"So you do like the idea of Seppa touching you?"

"I—I'm married to you."

He smiles and leans in to run his nose up the length of my neck. "That you are."

"So, I mean—"

"Seppa is very beautiful, my dear, it is more than understandable to like the idea of them fucking you."

"But I belong to you."

Fuck, I did not just say that.

"Oh, but you did," Jack answers my thoughts, his smile spreading across my skin as he does. "And you're right. You are mine. Which is why I get to decide who I share you with."

"What if I don't want to be shared?"

He slides his hand between my legs and my breath hitches a bit.

"But you do."

I do.

He pushes against the fabric of my dress to palm my pussy. I gasp and try to cover his hand with the folds of my skirt.

"Let them see, little will-o-wisp. Let them see who owns you."

He begins to rub his hand against my pussy, pressing his thumb into my clit so hard I can't hide the gasp that escapes my throat. I squirm against him as he continues and in response he wraps a hand around my stomach to hold me still.

I can't stop myself from glancing around at all the other revelers in the clearing, trying to gauge if anyone is watching us and wondering what they must think. Is voyeurism normal here? Is public sexual activity a respectable or deplorable thing?

"Calm that racing mind, little will-o-wisp," Jack whispers in my ear. "Focus on my fingers." He swirls his thumb against my clit harder and I whimper in response, my muscles relaxing just a little bit. "Good girl. Breathe. I've got you. Give me the chaos in your mind, I'll take care of it for you."

I lean my head back on his shoulder and give myself over to the extraordinary feeling of his fingers working me. He bites my neck and I moan, causing him to pick up the pace. Out of the corner of my eye I notice some of the revelers have turned in our direction and are taking in the sight of their king finger fucking his new queen.

"I would gladly share you with Seppa, my beautiful wife. Would it bring you pleasure to be filled in both your holes at once? Two tongues on you, four hands, endless pleasure."

"Yes," I breathe.

"There are so many Fae here who already lust after you. I can tell just by the way they look at you. They are all jealous that this wonderful little cunt is all mine. Isn't it, wife?"

He circles my clit even harder.

"Yes, husband," I pant, grinding against him, unable to help it.

"You want to cum, don't you?" He whispers in my ear.

"So badly," I whimper. "Please take me home."

Instead of answering me Jack shoots to his feet, knocking my dishes to the ground. He throws me over his shoulder yet again and all the other Folk cheer and whistle as he carries me off into the forest.

"You can't keep doing this," I huff once we're back in the cottage, the door barred, and me finally on my feet again.

He leans against the door and smirks.

"Can't I?"

He reaches forward and takes the crown from my head. He sets it down on top of the hearth, adding his next to it. He looks back and holds my gaze as he stalks over to me—an animal on the hunt.

"Take it out now," I say. "Please."

He looks me up and down.

"But I have such a better idea."

"Jack—"

I don't have time to finish my sentence before he's on me, his mouth crashing into mine as he spins me around and slams me against the wall, my palms smacking down hard enough to bruise. He bunches up my skirt and dips two fingers between my folds.

"You're soaked, wife."

"Yeah, unfortunately I'm attracted to my husband."

He laughs into the crook of my neck as he thrusts his cock deep inside me. My mouth falls open in a silent gasp at the feeling of being filled in each hole so intensely.

"When did you even take your icicle dick out?" I hiss as he moves in and out of me at a torturous pace.

He tugs on my hair, his sweet laughter still coating the air.

"I aim to always keep you on your toes, little will-o-wisp."

He rolls his hips against me and I groan, leaning back into his shoulder as his thrusts become faster and rougher.

"Listen to me," he says, leaning in closer so that his breath is cool on the back of my neck.

"What?" I gasp out as he keeps pounding into me with immense force.

"You are not just a toy."

He pulls out and I whimper in shock. I try to spin around to face him but he holds me still.

"Stop, my dear. Wait a moment."

He drops to his knees and snakes his hands up my thighs. I try to breathe evenly as he gently works the plug out of my ass. I exhale deeply in relief to have it gone, but not getting to finish (again) has left me with that awful empty feeling and I find I would rather have it back inside me than nothing at all right now.

Jack places the plug on the bedside table and walks back to me.

"Turn around."

I obey.

He cups my face in his cold hands.

"You are not a toy, you are my wife, my queen—you are *mine*. You belong to me and I take care of what's mine. Nothing I do or say is for show. You think me cruel because I do not care that you had no say in being here. Think that if you must. Attach your tiresome human morals to every-thing I do, but understand this, Mary Ellory Lark—I have waited years for you, I will not throw you away, I will not hurt you, and I will not let you go. So do not try again to escape me; I will never let you succeed. Do you understand?"

I hold his gaze for a moment, my rational sense of mind telling me to rail against every ridiculous alpha male thing he just said. But the rest of me is tired. Tired of being lonely. Of feeling unwanted. Of feeling used. Yes, my father sold me away to this creature, but this creature has shown more affection for me in the past twenty-four hours than anyone else has my entire life.

"Yes, husband. I understand."

He smiles at me. Not his mischievous smile but his pure one. His honest one.

"Good."

He steps back and begins to undo the laces of my stays. I keep my eyes locked with him as he helps me out of my clothes, and then as I help him out of his. He takes my glasses off and sets them aside before lifting me in his arms and carrying me over to the bed.

"I promise I will feed you after I've thoroughly fucked you."

He lays me down on the bed and just stands over me for a

moment, running his fingers up and down my leg, sending shivers all throughout my body.

"Jack," I whisper. "Please."

"Gods, I adore when you beg."

He crawls onto the bed and settles himself between my thighs. He kisses my mouth gently and then my chin and then my neck and soon he makes his way down to my breasts. He takes one nipple in his mouth and begins to suck and bite while he uses his fingers to pull and pinch the other. I moan in pleasure as I arch my back, pushing my breasts further into his mouth and hands. He switches and continues the wonderful torment all over again.

"Stunning," he murmurs as he kisses the spot between my breasts.

He starts kissing down my stomach until he makes his way to the hair above my sex. He tugs on it gently and chuckles appreciatively as I groan and squirm from the rough sensation. He dips his head down and drags a long lick through my folds from my asshole up to my clit. I whimper and arch against him but he grabs my hips, keeping me pinned to the bed.

"Let me work, wife."

"Jack," I breathe, barely able to form words, already so aroused from all the night's teasing.

"I know, Mary," he says.

He dips back down and pushes his tongue inside my pussy and I continue to moan as he fucks me with his mouth. Licking and sucking in all the right spots. Soon he releases his hold on my hips to use his fingers to circle my clit as he continues to push his tongue as deep as it can go. He keeps up the relentless pace as I writhe beneath him, moaning in pleasure.

"Jack, please."

He nips at my clit and I yelp.

"Please what, wife?"

"Please fuck me, husband."

"Hmmm."

He tugs on my pubic hair again and instead of doing what I beg for he continues to torture my pussy with licks and bites, continuously bringing me to the edge but never letting me fall over.

"Husband," I breathe, "please."

He laughs and plants one last kiss on my pussy before shifting up.

"Alright, my dear wife."

He kisses my mouth as he lines himself up with my entrance, slowly sinking into me.

I groan as his thick cock stretches me and fills me. I tilt my hips up to meet him, biting his bottom lip as I do.

"Gods, little will-o-wisp, fucking you is my new favorite thing."

Mine too.

"I heard that," he says with a smile against my mouth.

"I hate you," I whisper as he begins to move his hips slowly against mine.

He laughs and nips at my nose. "Liar."

He keeps fucking me slowly, tortuously, wonderfully. He feels so good it's disorienting. After a while, he starts to pick up the pace, thrusting his cock deeper and deeper into me; harder and harder, hitting all the spots that make me melt. He reaches one hand down between us to tease my clit as he picks up the pace of his thrusts. Eventually he's fucking me relentlessly and I can't help my moans.

"Scream for me, little will-o-wisp."

I do as he says, screaming as he pounds into me, impaling me on his icy cock again and again to bring me to a wonderful, blissful, maddening orgasm. With a loud groan he bites down on my neck and follows me over that precipice.

"On your stomach, wife," he commands.

I roll over and even though I know what's coming I still tense in surprise when I feel the tip of his shaft press against my ass.

"It's alright, my dear," he murmurs as he adds a significant amount of lube to my entrance.

He begins to circle me again with his finger, slipping in one and then two to help properly stretch me.

"I think I've punished this ass rather well," he says. "Now it's time I play with it, don't you agree, my wife?"

I turn and bury my face in the blankets as I groan. Jack lightly slaps my ass, causing me to jerk against him.

"Use your words, wife."

Yes, husband. I say in my mind. *Play with me.*

He begins to massage my ass cheeks in response and then he slowly works his cock inside me. I groan and tense again.

Breathe, little will-o-wisp.

I do as he says and soon the burning feeling of the invasion fades into a wonderful, stretched fullness that I never imagined I would enjoy.

"Mary," he murmurs as he drags a finger down my spine. "Monet means no."

"Monet means no," I say softly.

"I'm going to fuck you now."

"You are good at that," I say.

He laughs softly and then he pulls his shaft back out to the tip and slowly thrusts back into me. I lift my hips to take him in deeper and moan loudly as he begins to quicken his thrusts. He reaches a hand forward and presses his thumb to my clit and begins to circle it slowly again.

"Jack," I moan.

He's so big and my body is already so tender.

Hold on, my love, he says in my mind, answering my thoughts. *I can make you cum once more.*

And he's right. He picks up the pace, his thrusts becoming

more aggressive, the stretching, fullness more intense. I buck against his shaft and groan loudly as he manages to pull another orgasm from me. He starts tapping my clit like he did when we met and the light pressure combined with the intensity of him fucking my ass has me whimpering and writhing beneath him as I ride down the aftershocks of my orgasm. He too finishes with a groan and gently pulls out of me before wrapping me into a tight embrace.

We remain still in each other's arms for a few moments and then he slowly slides out of me and stands.

"Wait here."

I lay still as he walks to the kitchen and gets a cloth and walks over to a water basin in the corner where he wets it then walks back to me. He sits down on the side of the bed and gently rubs it over my breasts and between my legs.

"You don't have to do that," I say. "I've figured out by now that you don't ejaculate."

He smirks but continues his ministrations.

"This is true, but you produce a few fluids yourself, my dear. And I'm sure this pretty pussy is sore after being so used."

He presses the cloth flat against my mound and I whimper a bit.

"It is," I whisper.

"Umhm," he murmurs. "And I told you I take care of what's mine."

"You'll take care of me."

I don't pose it as a question but he answers me anyway.

"I will always take care of you, little will-o-wisp. Now, it's time for dinner."

He places the cloth at the end of the bed and stands to offer me his hand.

"I ate at the party."

"Earlier you badgered me for not feeding you. Get up."

This time I'm the one who smirks. I can't help it. With every passing hour I grow more and more at ease with him. It's like time is moving on overdrive. Humans don't usually marry someone less than an hour after meeting them and then spend almost every waking moment for the next night and day with them.

But apparently I'm not human at all. And as much as I loathe my father, this is what he bred me for, as he always said. I will hate him forever, but I spent so long fearing the worst would come when Jack Frost came to claim me, and now that he has and it isn't awful at all there is a sense of anxiety that has lingered over me all my life that can finally now fade away.

"Your mind is full of chaos again, my dear," Jack says as he leads me to the kitchen table and pulls out one of the two chairs for me.

"I'm just thinking."

He pushes in my chair and I try not to harp on the fact that we're both still nude. If I were back in the mortal realm I probably would have insisted we put on clothes. But all the old rules are out the window now.

"You mean you're worrying and over-analyzing," he says as he walks to the pantry.

"Oh, so you're an expert on ADHD now?"

"No, just my wife."

He takes two mugs off a shelf and a jar of tea leaves and sets them out on the counter.

"You met me yesterday," I say. "You're not an expert on me."

He fills the kettle with water and walks over to the fire to hang it over the flame. He saunters back over to me and I do my best to not stare at his cock as he does. He leans against the edge of the table and takes one of my hands in his. He brings it to his lips and plants a gentle kiss to the back of my knuckles then holds it with both of his. The entire thing is so gentle and caring that I don't know how to process it.

"I can be," he says. "But you are determined not to let me in."

"Can you blame me?" I ask softly. "I was raised on those morals you have such an issue with."

"But you weren't," he says, stroking the back of my hand with his thumb. "You were raised by your father. I did not know him long but it was more than enough to see his wickedness. I have no parents, but if I did I would pray they were nothing like your father."

"Shut up, Frost," I say. I try to pull my hand away but he doesn't let me.

"You can be sad that you had a bad life, Mary Ellory."

"It wasn't bad or good, it was just a life."

"Were you happy?" He asks.

"I just *was*. I don't know. Sometimes things were awful and sometimes they were fine and that's how it was. That's what human life is."

"You are not human."

"I know."

"Your father lied to you."

"Yes, great detective work, Frost."

He smirks and continues to stroke my hand.

"You hate him."

"I hate them all," I whisper.

"You said your father had many kids."

"Yeah, I have three brothers. And then I think two sisters, and another sibling or two, but I was only raised alongside my brothers. We all have different mothers. Different women from the settlement my father dragged back to his house. Occasionally women he met on drunken nights out in the city. I had assumed that's what my mother was. Some random, human woman who was unlucky enough to walk into my father's path."

"He is a wicked man," Jack says.

It's not a question but I nod anyway. "Not just him."

"Your brothers," he says.

I nod again. "I've had friends and coworkers over the years with siblings, they were friends. My brothers were not my friends. I was a joke. My father didn't plan any child's birth but mine, but I was not planned because I was wanted; I was needed. I'm a bargaining piece, a pawn moved around on the chessboard of somebody else's life. My brothers knew this and it was comical to them. Many of them possessed Elvish powers when I possessed none. And they all knew no matter what happened my entire life was decided for me."

"Not your entire life, little will-o-wisp," he says, softly.

I look into his icy eyes and fight the urge to cry.

"You might be the first man I've ever met who isn't awful."

He smiles at that, but it's not taunting.

"I told you, you didn't hate me."

"Shut up."

He smiles wider.

"It would have all been easier somehow if you had turned out to be as awful as I made you up to be in my head," I say.

"I'm sure that's true."

He reaches out and pushes a lock of hair behind my ear, but then changes his mind and brings it forward to twirl around his finger.

"Is blue your favorite color?"

"Yes. That's an incredibly shallow question, what is this—our first date?"

He laughs again and drops my hair to reach down and pinch one of my nipples. I gasp and lean back but he holds on.

"We are far past that, my dear."

I slap his hand away and his beautiful laugh fills the air again.

"What are you afraid of, Mary Ellory?"

"Nothing."

"Liar."

"What are you afraid of, Jack Frost?"

"Fire."

"But—" I glance at the hearth where the kettle is boiling water and then back at him. "Are you being serious right now?"

He nods as he begins to run his fingers up and down my neck.

"You know the folktale, don't you? The legend of Lemminkäinen."

"I do. But I didn't think it was literal."

"It was more or less so."

"Doesn't all of this contradict with science?"

"Science is just the magic humans have figured out."

I sit back in my chair, but he just leans forward to keep touching my neck. I look at the fire again. "Why do you have that then?"

"For you."

I look back at him in surprise.

"There was no fireplace in this cottage until you came. I had Cilla speak to some of the other Folk to have it arranged. I knew even with my ice you could still get cold and I knew you would need fire for meals and I wasn't about to figure out how to get electricity. That is a magical science I have no desire to tamper with."

"I—" I look away again at the fire, at a loss for what to say in the face of this kindness. I finally look back at him. "Can you tamper with the magic to have running water?"

He smirks. "We will see."

We sit in silence for a few moments. The only sound is the fire crackling and the snow falling outside.

"I was afraid of you," I finally admit. "A part of me still is."

"Because I bought you."

"Because...you said it yourself, winter kills. And yes, you bargained away a gift and took payment in the form of a woman."

"You're right. Winter kills. But I don't. I do not cause death. Humans exert their will and I am one of many who shows up to pick up the pieces. I bring snow and ice and storms when it is called upon, when it is needed, when the land in the human realm can handle it. What they do with my gifts is not my problem."

"But you bargain. In the story of Lemminkäinen the farmer summoned you, bargained with you to have you freeze the hero's ship and his crew."

"She did."

"My father summoned you."

"Yes."

"Why?" I ask, my voice sounding more desperate than I like. "Why do you do it?"

"Because I like to. I have been around for centuries, ever since the God and Goddess of The Forest decided they were tired from worrying about the mortal realm and their weather. They birthed myself and my three sibling counterparts into existence and left us to deal with it all. Winter is such a small snapshot in the grand scheme of a lifetime. I get bored, and mortals are even more boring. Toying with them is entertaining."

"Toying with me is entertaining."

My voice comes out as a whisper and I silently curse myself for not being smarter. For letting myself fall for him so quickly. I tilt my head down, unable to hold his intense stare any longer.

"Tormenting you and teasing you and fucking you is entertaining," he says, grabbing my chin in his thumb and forefinger and forcing me to look up at him. "I did not bargain in return for a wife as a game. I did it because I wanted a wife. I wanted *you*."

I stare into his fierce blue eyes for a small eternity and decide to hope with everything I have that this is true. That he's not lying. That he's not playing the iconic trickster he's famously known to be. I decide to put my faith in him to be honest with me.

"Okay," I say softly.

He smiles, then releases my chin and gets up to get the tea kettle.

CHAPTER 4

Blizzard

I wake up to Jack's tongue deep in my pussy. I moan softly as I tilt my hips up towards his mouth. He digs his fingers into my hips as he nuzzles further into my folds.

"Jack," I breathe.

He practically growls against me as he shifts to release one of my hips and insert two fingers inside me, crooking them just right to hit my G-spot causing me to cry out in ecstasy.

It's been several days since Jack first brought me here and nearly every morning this is how he wakes me and I never get tired of it.

He keeps tongue fucking me until I finish with another loud cry and a hand fisted in his hair. He gives me one final lick then moves up to kiss me, the taste of my pleasure still wet on his lips.

"Good morning, dear wife."

"Good morning, husband."

"I have work to do today. I won't be done until later I'm afraid."

"Did Frosty lose his hat again?"

Jack smiles and bites my shoulder lightly.

"No, dear," he says, licking up my neck. "A snowstorm in England. Boring stuff. Seppa and Cilla added new books to your library."

"Am I to read everyday while I await you to come home from your wintery duties for all eternity?"

"Was there something else you wanted to do?" he asks, genuinely sounding curious.

I prop myself up on my elbows and he rests his head on my stomach, looking up at me with those beautiful blue eyes.

"I don't know. I'm the queen but I don't feel like I do anything very queenly."

"Admittedly, my dear, this isn't Faerie, our politics are much more tame. They're rather nonexistent really."

"I want to *do* something, Jack."

He sits up and back on his knees. He reaches out for my hands and I let him take them, pulling me up to sit. He cups my face in his hands the way he likes and smiles down at me.

"You should learn to paint."

"What?"

"You like looking at paintings so much. Maybe making them would help with the chaos." He taps my forehead when he says this. "I've decided!"

He jumps up and heads across the room to the wardrobe.

"Jack, I don't know."

"Nonsense! Cilla can paint. I'll send her by."

"No," I insist, following him out of bed. "I'll go to her. I don't want to spend all day here without you."

He strides over to me, now fully dressed in his normal tight pants and flowing shirt getup, and kisses me.

"Very well. I will have her come get you and bring you to her lodgings. Until tonight, my love."

He kisses me once more and then he's gone.

I get dressed and wait for Cilla. Fifteen minutes later she glides through the door, looking as stunning as ever.

"Good morning, my Queen."

"Cilla, just call me Mary."

Cilla gives me one of her cunning smiles.

"Very well, Mary Ellory. Your husband says you wish to paint?"

"I do, I guess. Couldn't hurt to try, right?"

She takes my hand in hers and starts dragging me out the door without saying anything else. We walk for a short while through the forest until we reach what appears to be a small village. There are several houses, and a few buildings that look more official. The whole thing looks like a Thomas Kincaid painting.

"Where are we?" I ask.

"The Winter Village," she says.

"Who lives here?"

"Myself. Seppa. Some of the other Folk who are particularly close with the King, or easily lonely elsewhere. Come."

She still holds my hand as she drags me onward into the village. A few folk are outside their homes or walking to and fro and they bow to me as Cilla and I walk by, saying *My Queen* as they do. I wonder if I'll ever get used to that.

A little ways further and Cilla stops outside a rosy colored house with a garden outside that seems to defy the snow that keeps falling on it.

"Flower enchantment," she says, smiling proudly. "Took me centuries to master. Come inside, Seppa is waiting."

"Seppa is here?" I haven't seen Seppa since my coronation and I'm admittedly nervous to see them again after all the erotic images Jack put in my head about them.

"We live together," Cilla says, coolly as she waltzes up the steps into the house.

I follow after her and am struck dumb upon entering. Every wall is covered with the most beautiful murals of the Winter Forest. Cilla walks over to one of the far walls that looks like a giant window covered in intricate frost patterns and swirls.

"Your husband did this one."

"Jack can paint?"

"When he can manage to sit still long enough," Seppa says as they enter the room, shirtless, paint smeared across their face, chest, and hands. "Hello, my Queen, welcome to our home."

"You can just call me Mary."

"Our King calls her Mary Ellory," Cilla says.

I sigh.

"Mary Ellory," Seppa repeats with a beautiful smile. "Ready to learn?"

I look back at Jack's stunning painting, surprised by my husband yet again.

"I suppose so."

Several hours later and my hands are sore from gripping the brush and my fingers and forehead are streaked with paint. I step back from my canvas and examine my spruce tree. It kind of sucks, but it's better than the first three I managed.

"It's not terrible," Cilla says as she steps up right behind me. She reaches up and pushes my hair over my shoulder. "It will get better with practice."

She presses two of her fingers to my spine and begins to gently drag them down my back. I go still at her touch and hold my breath.

"Cilla," I breathe. I glance over at Seppa, they're watching with rapt and ravenous eyes.

"It's alright, my Queen," she murmurs in my ear. "Your husband said we could."

"I—"

Before I can say anything else Cilla's mouth is on my neck, stealing the words from my mouth. She grazes my skin with her teeth, flicking her tongue across the spot and I close my eyes and moan softly as her hands go to my hips, pulling me back to her.

"My Queen."

I open my eyes to see Seppa standing before me, their gold eyes gazing down into mine.

"May I?"

I nod wordlessly.

Seppa smiles and leans down to press their mouth to mine. They taste like lemon and mint and it's delicious. They press their tongue to the seam of my lips and I open to let them in. They begin to invade my mouth with sensual swirls of their tongue, drawing another moan from me. All while Cilla kisses and bites her way up and down my neck, her nails scraping against my hips.

I see you started playing without me.

"Jack!"

I break free of the couple's embrace to turn and see my husband standing in the doorway, leaning up against the frame with a wicked smile on his lips.

"Keep going," he says softly. "I like watching you two undo her."

Jack takes a step forward as Cilla and Seppa return to their attentions, their mouths and hands exploring my body.

"Take off her clothes," Jack instructs.

Seppa and Cilla make quick work of doing away with my dress and stays until I'm wearing nothing but paint.

"Please," I beg against Seppa's mouth.

"My wife is a needy one," Jack says as I hear his footsteps get closer.

"Would you like us to give her what she needs, my King?" Cilla asks.

"No, I will. You two play with her breasts."

I open my mouth to speak but then Jack thrusts two fingers inside me as his hand knots in my hair at the base of my neck, pulling me back and causing me to moan yet again. Cilla and Seppa do as he commands and begin to play with my nipples. Plucking and twisting and tugging, causing me to squirm and whine. I have never experienced so much pleasure all at once and it is a terrible bliss.

"Seppa," Jack says.

"Yes, my King?"

"Smack her clit."

"Jack—" I start but then Seppa's hand slaps down hard on my clit while Cilla takes over tugging on my nipples and Jack is still finger fucking me and I scream and buck against all the hands on me, unable to contain all the pleasure.

"Too much," I pant.

"Oh, my dear wife," Jack says, leaning in close to whisper in my ear. "It's not nearly enough."

Jack adds a third finger as Seppa continues to lightly spank my pussy and Cilla takes one of my nipples in her mouth. I lean my head back against Jack's shoulder and groan, the sensations overwhelming me.

"Seppa," Jack says again, "I think I'm going to need your help filling up my wife."

"Gladly, my King."

"Excellent."

Cilla and Seppa suddenly remove their hands from me and step back as Jack picks me up and throws me over his shoulder as he likes to do. He carries me up the stairs with Cilla and Seppa in tow behind us. We reach a bedroom and Jack places me down gently on the bed and then begins to undress. Cilla and Seppa enter the room and do the same.

Soon three stunning Folk stand before me.

"You're beautiful," I whisper.

Cilla smiles as she walks over to the bed and straddles me.

"I know."

She slides my glasses off my nose and sets them aside before swooping down to claim my mouth in a kiss so fierce and passionate it makes my head spin. She holds my face still as she ravages my mouth, dragging moan after moan from my lips.

"Cilla," Jack commands, "share."

Cilla pulls back, grinning down at me.

"Apologies, my King."

She climbs off me and Jack takes her place. He reaches down and presses his palm along the curve of my jaw, I lean into the touch.

"Hello," I say softly.

He smiles. "Hello, wife."

"Please fuck me, husband."

His smile widens as he leans down to kiss me.

"You know I love when you beg."

He presses his lips to mine, wasting no time in shoving his own tongue inside my mouth and it is better than the rest. I reach up and tangle my hands in his blonde hair, pulling slightly. He groans softly against my lips and I feel a small surge of pride at the sound.

"Ready?" He whispers against my lips.

I nod.

"Good girl."

Jack gets up and flips us over so that I'm straddling him, his thick length pressing between my lips already soaked in arousal. Seppa climbs on the bed behind me and squirts some lube into their hand. Cilla presses a hand to my back to push me forward. I lean down and kiss my husband as he lifts my hips and begins to impale me with his cock.

"Jack," I moan against my mouth.

"Mary," he whispers back.

Seppa spreads me from behind and lathers my tight entrance with lube and then I feel their cock press up against me. It's not as big as Jack's but it's still large and I tense up on instinct.

"Come now, wife," Jack whispers in my ear as he slowly pumps into me. "You took my cock with ease, you can take Seppa's."

"Okay," I whisper back.

"Good girl," he says again.

Seppa begins to press into me and I groan from the intensity of fullness that comes with the welcome intrusion.

"Breathe, my love," Jack says, his hips still thrusting into me.

"You're stunning, my Queen," Seppa says as they push all the way in until they're seated fully in my ass.

I groan and let my head fall forward to rest on Jack's shoulder.

"It's okay," Jack says.

I nod against him and then the two begin to move and there is really nothing I can do but take it. It's intense and wonderful and horrible and I can't stop the moans and mewls that keep coming forth from my mouth as the two rail me aggressively and passionately. It doesn't take long for my orgasm to start building up, begging to be released.

"My King?" Cilla asks.

"Yes, of course," Jack replies.

Then Cilla's hands are on my breasts again, tugging at my nipples so hard I cry out. Cilla just smiles as I do; the viciousness of a fairy.

"Lovely," she says as I writhe and moan.

The three of them continue to fuck me relentlessly; tormenting and torturing every part of me with beautiful pleasure. I want to cum so badly but they keep bringing me to the edge only to bring me back down before I can topple over.

"Jack," I moan.

"Yes, my little will-o-wisp?"

"Please."

"You know the rule, my dear."

I let my head loll back as he and Seppa keep pounding into me, spearing me on their cocks as Cilla moves her fingers down to circle my clit ferociously.

"Please let me cum, husband."

"Gladly."

Jack and Seppa and Cilla all pick up the pace, fucking me so intensely that I scream like I've been stabbed as my orgasm claims me. I collapse against my husband as I finish and his arms wrap tightly around me as Cilla and Seppa remove themselves.

"Leave us," Jack commands.

"My King, my Queen," they say in unison before retreating and leaving us alone in the room.

"What—" I start, my head still pressed to his chest, "—the fuck was that?"

"Did you like it?"

"Obviously."

He chuckles and kisses the top of my head.

"Take me home, please," I say.

"Of course, my love."

He reaches over for my glasses and slides them back onto my face. Then he scoops me up into his arms and carries me down the stairs and out the door.

"Jack! Our clothes!"

"We have more at the cottage. Besides, your dress was covered in paint. Cilla will clean it and bring it back."

"We can't walk through The Forest naked!" I protest.

"Of course we can, it's mine. As are you."

"Yes, you like to remind me of that."

"I just like to say it."

I don't respond to that, just nestle against him and allow myself to be carried home. Once we reach the cottage he sets me on the bed and goes to make tea. A short while later he returns to me with a cup of the chocolate-chip cookie flavored beverage. I take the cup and sip hungrily.

"Did you have fun?" he asks as he reaches out and traces his finger along my knee.

"Yes. I already told you I did."

He laughs. "I meant the painting."

"Oh, yeah I did. I suck at it but it's only day one. I'll get there."

He smiles and continues to trace patterns along my thigh.

"I saw your painting," I say after a tentative silence. "The frost swirls and patterns." I wait for him to respond but he doesn't, just keeps his hand steady and his eyes locked on mine. "It's beautiful," I say.

He smiles and I love it.

"You're not as wicked as I thought," I say.

He throws his head back and laughs and then brings me close to kiss me, the taste of cookies on our tongues.

"And you, Mary Ellory Lark, are even more wonderful than I ever could have hoped."

CHAPTER 5

Eye of The Storm

"Do you miss the human realm?" Cilla asks me as we're painting for the sixth day in a row.

I look up from my canvas where my spruce is finally starting to resemble a tree and over to where she leans against the wall, looking at me over the top of her own canvas.

"A little. But I've started accepting that I can't ever really go back so it's best not to harp on it."

"Why can't you go back?" She asks, her voice almost taunting. "Your big bad husband won't let you?"

Confused, I hold up one of my arms, showing off the ice forever stained on my skin.

"I'll die if I leave this realm without him, and he's made it pretty clear he only goes there when it's time to change the seasons or he's specifically summoned."

Cilla smirks at me, sets her paintbrush down on her easel and saunters over to stand before me.

"Who told you that you'll die if you leave the Winter Forest without him?"

Oh Gods.

"You mean—"

Cilla reaches out and pushes a lock of hair behind my ear.

"Jack Frost is a notorious trickster, surely you know that, little goblin girl."

"But—" the room tilts on its axis.

"He had you *bred* into existence. The girl made of elf and goblin heritage; blood strong enough to withstand him. He made sure you were perfect for him the day he bought your unborn soul from your fool father. But your stupid father raised you as well as if you were human. Do you really think a girl with blood as magical as yours can't cross the barriers between the worlds on her own?"

I feel like I'm going to throw up.

"The real shame of it all is—" Cilla gets up and starts walking back to her own easel, "—it looks like you've grown to love him. What a pity."

I stand up, the stool I've been sitting on falling over, and I race out the door without even stopping to grab my cloak. I hear Cilla laughing behind me but I ignore her. I race down the steps of her house and collide into Seppa.

"My Queen," they say, holding me steady. "What's wrong?"

"Seppa, can I leave The Winter Forest?"

"Pardon?"

"Will it kill me to leave on my own?"

"Of course not," they say, honest confusion painted across their eyes. "Why would you think that?"

"Oh my Gods," I whisper and then I take off running.

Seppa calls after me but I ignore them.

It takes me far too long to reach the clearing where the portal to Boston shimmers in the air.

Little will-o-wisp, Jack says in my head, *I'm at Cilla's, where did you go?*

I don't answer, I do my best to think thoughts of anything but what I'm about to do and then I run through the portal.

I come tumbling out on the museum floor in the middle of the night.

"Who's there?" the voice of what must be the new night-time security guard calls out.

It's fine, let me be another ghost, I certainly look the part. I get up and start heading for the back door.

Welcome back, Mary, ghost girl whispers.

I flip off the air and flee the museum.

Of course the first person I run into on the windy Boston streets is Crazy Hettie.

"Mary!" she calls out as she comes rushing over to me. "How did you get back?"

"Fuck off, Hettie," I grumble as I wrap my arms around my torso to try and keep warm. "I'm going home."

"Where's Frost?"

"There's no such thing as Jack Frost," I snap at her. "He's a stupid fucking legend my father made up. Now go home."

I move on, walking briskly and ignoring Hettie as she shouts after me. I ignore the confused looks of late night partiers stumbling home from various pubs, I ignore the bite in the wind, and I ignore the ache in my heart.

He lied.

Of course he lied.

I was so stupid to think he wouldn't. It took only a little over a week for The Winter King to make me his own and convince me he actually cared about me.

I shuffle on as snow begins to fall. I know it's him trying to deter me, but I'm a goddamn Bostonian born and raised, if anyone can withstand a little snow, it's me.

I make it to my tiny studio apartment and find the extra key I kept hidden beneath a loose floorboard in the hall. I'm barely two steps in the door before a Jack grabs me, clamping a hand down on my mouth and slamming the door shut.

"You just can't fucking behave, can you?" he hisses in my ear.

I try to speak against the firm grip he has over my mouth but it's no use.

He drags me over to the kitchen counter and slams me down across it, my cheek pressing into the cool surface, my glasses tilting askew. Jack bunches up my dress around my hips and spanks me hard.

I cry out. But he keeps doing it.

"Why would you worry me like this, Mary? Why!"

His spanking becomes too much to take. It's not fun and playful like it has been in the past, it's too heavily mixed with sadness and anger. This isn't how it's supposed to be between us.

"Monet!" I scream.

He immediately stops and helps me stand up. He gently holds my face, bending down a bit to meet my stare then he gently removes my glasses and sets them on the counter before pulling me into an embrace. He wraps his arms around my back as I sigh in defeat of so many kinds and rest my head on his chest.

"What the hell were you thinking?" he asks, smoothing a hand down my hair. "I had no idea where you went, you could've been hurt."

"Winter *is* brutal," I mutter.

He pulls me back and holds me at arms' length, looking intensely at me again.

"What the hell does that mean?"

"You lied to me."

A horrible silence sits between us.

"I *can* leave The Winter Forest without you. You lied, Jack Frost."

His fingers dig into my arms as frustration and anger seeps into his eyes again.

"Do you want me to apologize?"

"Yes," I whisper.

"Well that would be a lie. Because I'm not sorry I did it."

"Jack—"

"I'm not," he insists. "I waited years for you, I wasn't going to risk losing you. I don't care if it hurts you now to hear this, but you were always meant to be mine, Mary Ellory. You were meant to eat at my table, and ride my cock, and sleep in my arms. You. Are. *Mine.*"

"What about what I want!" I shout. "It can't all be destiny and fate. I'm a person. I should be your partner, not your possession."

"Is that truly what you want?" He says, his voice condescending.

"Yes," I say, but it comes out soft and weak.

He laughs and digs his fingers in deeper.

"But it's not. I can hear every thought in your head, my little will-o-wisp. I know when you're lying and you're lying right now. You don't want a partner, you want someone to take care of you, to fight for you and adore you, to tell you what to do. You spent your whole life alone, even when you were surrounded by other people. No one cared deeply and passionately about you until me. No one was willing to die for you until me. No one gave a shit if you were happy until me. And you know that and I *know* you feel that. You don't want to be someone's equal partner, you want to be someone's prized possession, someone's muse, someone's reason for breathing. You want someone to make all your decisions for you because they know what will make you the happiest because they *know* you, because you are theirs. Tell me I'm wrong, Mary."

I fight back a sob. His words hurt because they are so brutally true.

"You're not wrong, Jack."

"Then why did you run from me?"

I pause. All games have winners.

"Because I wanted you to chase after me."

There is another moment of silence and then he nods once.

"I thought so."

Jack reaches up and cups the back of my neck as he brings his mouth down to mine. The kiss is bruising and desperate and I let myself get lost in it. I wrap my arms around his neck as he picks me up and sits me down on the counter. He pauses his kisses for a moment and just rests his forehead against mine.

"Say Monet, little will-o-wisp."

"No," I whisper, pressing a gentle kiss to his nose. "Not this time. But—" I reach down and grab his balls roughly in my hand and squeeze, he groans and twitches against me. "If you ever spank me without the purpose of making me cum again I will cut out your heart and eat it for breakfast. Do you hear me, Winter King?"

His wicked smile spreads across my lips as he grips my neck tightly.

"Every word, my Queen, now let me fuck you."

I release his balls and spread my legs wide.

"With pleasure."

Jack quickly undoes the laces of his pants, letting his wonderful icy cock spring free. He lines himself up with my entrance, bunching my dress up around my hips, and then he thrusts into me with ease.

"You're so wet for me already, my dear wife."

I kiss him and moan into his mouth as he thrusts into my tight cunt.

"Well, sadly I like you."

He plants another marvelously violent kiss to my lips. "Lucky me."

"Yes, lucky you, Frost."

He laughs and bites my lower lip hard enough to draw blood. I slap him playfully at the pain and he laps up the blood.

"Is that the best you can do, husband?" I ask, tilting my hips a bit closer to his.

"Oh, my darling wife, you haven't seen the worst of me yet."

I lean forward and bite his lip. "Prove it, Frost."

With a primal growl he drags me off the counter and slams me down on the floor, pushing me up onto my hands and knees. I breathe shallowly from excitement as he presses the head of his cock up against my slick folds and roughly slams into me. I groan loudly in sheer euphoria as he continues to pound into me again and again, impaling me on that glorious cock.

He reaches forward and knots his hand in my hair and tugs until my head is tilted back and with the other hand he reaches around and wraps it around my throat, applying enough pressure to make me gasp.

"Say Monet," he pants as his hips slam into mine.

"No," I say back.

He tightens his grip on my throat and picks up the pace, his thrusts getting more and more aggressive.

"Gods, you're perfect," he murmurs as he fucks me so hard I see stars.

"Let me cum, husband."

"Always, wife."

He thrusts into me with all his strength and I cry out in bliss as my orgasm takes me. Jack groans loudly and follows me over the edge. The two of us collapse to the floor in a beautiful heap of sweaty limbs. He wraps me in his arms and pulls me close.

"Don't lie to me ever again," I say. "Or I will leave you and never come back."

"I won't ever let you leave again," he says. He taps a finger to my forehead. "Without me, who else will keep this chaos under control?"

I playfully nip at his finger and he laughs before pressing another kiss to my lips.

"Come home with me, wife," he whispers against my mouth. "Come back to your forest and be our queen." He kisses me again, and it is the gentlest, most loving kiss he's ever given me. "Come home and be mine forever."

I kiss him back.

"Forever," I agree.

CHAPTER 6

Winter Winds

"I love watching the meteorologists scramble to make sense of my mess," Jack calls out as he walks in the door to the cottage.

His eyes are down as he walks to the kitchen table and puts down a basket filled with cookies and candies and other treats I demanded he get from the human world while he was there wreaking havoc.

"Jack," I say.

He looks up at me and smiles.

"You look beautiful," he says, taking in my long silver dress I had Cilla design with his frost patterns along the fabric.

"I have something for you."

He grins as he walks over and puts his hands on my hip.

"What is it?"

I step back and gesture to the bed. He looks past me and his eyes go wide in shock. I grin in delight that I am finally able to surprise him.

"Mary," he says softly.

Above the bed, hanging next to Haystacks at Dusk, is the painting I've been working on for months. Jack releases me and walks over to the painting. He reaches up and gently touches it before turning back around to look at me, sparkles in his eyes.

"It's our wedding night."

I look up at my work; a painting of the spruce we stood under the night we were wed three months ago, snow glittering on the branches, sparkles all along my dress. We stand before it in the painting, hands locked as Jack's ice spreads up my arms.

"Is this what you've been working on with Cilla all this time?"

I nod. "It is."

"I—" he looks at it again. "You've bested me this time, my dear wife. I don't know what to say."

"Yes, you do."

He turns back to face me and his wonderful, wicked grin reappears. He strides back across the cottage and sweeps me up in his arms as he kisses me. I kiss him back as I tangle my hands in his hair, drinking down the taste of him.

"You're right," he says against my lips. "I know exactly what to say." He looks deep into my eyes. "I love you, Mary Ellory Lark."

I smile at him and for one glorious moment everything is right in the realm.

"I love you too, Jack Frost."

Acknowledgments

Thank you to Lady Marcia for dusting this story with your magic the way the world is dusted with snow during the winter.

Thank you to Karolyn Haines for crafting a beautiful cover that transcends being just a romance cover and is truly a work of art.

Thank you to Katy Doyle for proofreading this tale and making sure the grammar was correct.

Thank you to everyone in the Magical Molly discord server for always being a supportive and bright light in my creative endeavors,

Thank you to my incredible readers.

And finally, thank you to my mother, the reason any of this is possible.

Molly Likovich is the author of *Riding The Headless Horseman,* its sequel *Getting With The Ghoul,* as well as titles such as *Send in The Clowns* and *There's Something in The Woods.* She is the co-author of *Not a Myth* and *The Willow's Silence.* She is also an accomplished poet with a BA in Creative Writing from Salisbury University. She can currently be found frolicking around the forest somewhere.

Also by Molly Likovich

Riding The Headless Horseman (Sexy Sleepy Hollow #1)

Getting With The Ghoul (Sexy Sleepy Hollow #2)

Send in The Clowns

There's Something in The Woods

Loved Alone

Be Terrible

Lumos & Lattes